THE WINTER MOON'S WOLF

DIANA DERICCI

Purple Sword Publications
Tucson, AZ

THE WINTER MOON'S WOLF
Copyright © 2015 DIANA DERICCI
ISBN 978-1-61292-141-9
ISBN 10: 1612921418
Cover Art Designed by Anastasia Rabiyah
Edited by Traci Markou

Published by Purple Sword Publications, LLC
Tucson, Arizona, USA
www.PurpleSword.com

The Silo Series
Reading List:

Run with the Moon
Healed Beginnings
The Winter Moon's Wolf

Chapter One

Old country roads. Country music. Cade almost flinched. *No.* Grind. Extreme metal. Make his ears bleed industrial. That was what he needed. He found it and cranked the stream through the audio system.

Cade crowded over the handlebars, riding the Fat Bob low and fast. Bitterly cold air smacked at exposed skin as he raced through the night. His cheeks and hands quickly felt chapped, the icy air stinging. At least he could feel it. He'd felt numb from the inside out for weeks, maybe months. He'd lost track.

Sprinkled stars glittered overhead. Wisps of clouds were random thin trails that sliced the sky. The road lay like a river of unpolished onyx, broken only by the safety lines being eaten by the motorcycle's tires.

But it suited his mood. He was looking for someone to pick a fight tonight. Fuck, he *needed* someone to pick a fight.

A replay of the evening spent with his brothers broke the hold of his burgeoning anger. Christmas craziness wall to wall. It hadn't been a bad night, but everything about him felt…*off.*

Chris and Jamie. Quade and Maya. Fuck, even Ed was with Duncan. Now if that wasn't a kick in the fucking nut sac. After meeting Duncan the first time, Cade had been sure the man was going to prove everyone right and fuck up Ed something bad. Even he could see Duncan was a walking commitment-phobe. They'd looked pretty damn cozy tonight.

He growled low in his throat. He *knew* it wasn't Duncan's about-face that he couldn't understand. No. If Ed could tame the wildness in Duncan, then more power to him.

Cade knew what was really eating his ass alive. *Quade.*

His twin had found his mate. And not just a brainless joke with tits, either. The woman had brains that could probably write circles around Cade. The one thing he'd always had on his twin was he knew he was better, smarter, more...

Until now. He'd found his mate first. And in words only a brother could use safely, she was fucking fantastic.

He bared his teeth to the night, challenging it. None of the Rose boys were short on ambition, but there'd always been this little something *more* between Cade and Quade. A constant battle.

Jamie thought he was pining over a woman. Cade wished he were! He would have barked a laugh outright if he hadn't needed all his focus to control the bike. There wasn't so much as a date, much less a girlfriend in his life right now. That was part of the whole problem. He hadn't found a woman in years who really got to him, and none had so much as earned a sniff from his wolf. And now he was gnashing his teeth in frustration.

He didn't know where he was going and didn't really care. He'd driven home after the Christmas party and hadn't bothered to go in, grabbing his bike from the side garage and tearing like the devil were on his heels out of Silo. It was too cold to be out on the street demon, but Cade honestly couldn't find it in him to give a shit.

As fury simmered under the surface, feeling the bluster of winter cold was the least of his concerns. He'd been trying for weeks to get his head on straight. To find an outlet for his torment.

Ever since his brother had brought home Maya... The minute Cade met her, he *knew*. Whether Quade had told her everything then or not, it hadn't mattered. She was his. Which left Cade last. Again.

His growl was almost louder than the machine. *Almost.*

He opened the throttle a little more, hearing the whine of the engine as it thrummed like a rocket between his legs.

What he needed was a good old fashioned bar fight. It shouldn't matter that Quade had found his woman first. Saying it and believing it though...

Eventually, he slowed the machine. Lights in the distance said a town wouldn't be too far up the road. Towns meant cops. He definitely didn't want a ticket. Sitting straight, he cupped a hand and blew into it, giving it a modicum of warmth. He'd regret not having his gloves, but when this cold would be causing major issues with anyone else, all he had was frigid skin and stiff fingers from keeping the bike under control.

Another mile or so dropped him into Podunk Country. A small barn-cum-bar was lit up with spotlights in the parking lot, the building surrounded by vehicles, a majority pickup trucks. He felt his smile grow a little wickeder.

Gemini's. Suddenly, he was really thirsty for a beer.

He hoped the holiday revelers were ready for him.

Cruising into the lot, he found a spot to park and slid off the seat. Pocketing his keys, he took a moment to take in the surroundings. He wasn't on a neighboring pack's territory. That made him feel better. He didn't want to invade on another pack's grounds, especially not if he was looking for a fight.

Because that was exactly what he was looking for.

It looked like any other country dive walking in. Only now it was festooned with all kinds of garish seasonal markers. Tinsel hung from various places around the bar, glittering in the offset lights overhead. A string of colored tree bulbs framed the top liquor rack. In other words, as little effort as possible to barely scrape past pointless to skid right into tacky. The bar was busy considering the next day was Christmas Eve. A jukebox played a twang-y Christmas carol. Cade gritted his teeth at the cosmic yodel from Hell.

It was probably doing the wrong kind of job for him. Instead of making him feel nostalgic, he wanted to bash heads — right into that machine would be a great place to start.

He didn't exactly ask for permission headed through the crowd for the bar, cutting between people with barely a dropped snarl. At six-three, very few could look down on him. In black leather, with his hair tied back, he didn't look approachable. And that was fine with him.

When he reached the bar, he leaned an elbow on the scarred wood and stared at the bartender until he got service.

"What'll i'be? It's almost last call," the man warned.

"Dark ale. Warm." He hated being served ales out of the cooler. *So wrong.*

He got a grunt and an arched eyebrow in answer. When the beer appeared he put his money down. Holding it in his warming hands, it didn't feel iced. Glad to know he found someone who can listen *and* deliver.

He didn't face the crowd, leaning over an elbow instead to face the rear wall. He cocked a foot on the floor rail and drank his beer in slow drags. Cade may have looked undisturbed and uninterested to the night's festivities, but all anyone had to do was watch his gaze in the mirror hanging on the wall.

Something niggled at him, poked at him, but he ignored it. A scent maybe. Something that told him he should be paying attention. Instead he watched the crowd. He knew what he *needed* to be aware of. Energy coursed through his body, building with power as more added to it, increasing his anticipation like runoff hitting a roaring river. He controlled it.

For now.

Most of the crowd were young bucks. Country boys in cowboy hats. He sneered silently. He was only a few years older than those same high on life idiots at twenty-eight. They might even be the same age, but all they shared was the number. He'd never brayed like that in public. He shook his head at the brazen catcalls being tossed around. Cade wanted a good old-fashioned fight, but he wasn't going to fight guys who were so drunk, they didn't know if they were asses, or people. There weren't many women in the crowd. He doubted they'd be caught dead at this hour in this madness.

He finished his beer and ordered another.

"Last one. Last call!" the bartender shouted into the melee after pocketing Cade's bills.

"Fuck you, Dean!"

"Shove it!" he barked. "My bar. It's closing time!"

"Gonna call the wah-wahambulance if we stay?" A crowd of about seven or so jeered in support.

"No, I'll call the cops. Finish your drinks and get out of here." He flipped a bar rag over his shoulders, shaking his head. "Damn kids. They turn twenty-one and become everything Mom warned me about."

Cade huffed, sipping his beer. He was studying the situation. He might just get the chance to expend some of his inner energy if Blotto Jr. and his pals started giving the bartender bullshit.

"You the only one working tonight?" he asked.

Dean flicked a quick glance to Cade. "Yeah. Wasn't expecting them." He jerked his head toward the asinine fools. "Gave Garret the night off to be with his family. Closed for the next three days." He crossed his arms and continued to watch the milling crowd as they got louder and rowdier over something as strenuous as having to obey the law at closing time.

Cade saluted him with the bottle and then drew a sip. He waited, patiently, as the clock ticked down. He didn't want to cause issues for Dean if he could handle this on his own, but by the building momentum the party boys were gathering, Cade had a hell of a feeling deep in his gut that this wasn't going to be a good night for the birthday boy.

When he finished the last of the ale, he licked his lip and pushed the empty toward the trench edge.

He stood from the bar and sauntered like he owned the place across the room heading for the restroom. A good piss. That should take about ten minutes if he stopped to read the writing on all the walls. He gave the crowing group another half glance.

They were going to be trouble.

He smirked, biting his lips to hide the cold smile.

He could hardly wait.

* * * *

Dean saw the man straighten and walk like a fucking god across the room. He was huge, tall, thick, and gorgeous. And jee-*sus*. But did his hair reach the middle of his back? He had it tied into a ponytail, and it swayed like one. He dared a peek south and groaned. The man's ass was dream inducing. In black denim, beneath black leather, two perfectly rounded sides. Dean bit his cheek to not moan in appreciation.

Not that it would be heard, but still. He didn't let on to his preferences at work, though it wasn't a huge secret. There simply hadn't been an *other half* in his life in a long time.

Another cheer snapped his attention to the open floor. He was considering calling the cops for backup, regardless. He was only one man and while there had been a lot of people there tonight, last call had quickly started the exodus for the night. Most evenings he didn't have a problem running solo.

Tonight looked to be one of those nights that went against the grain.

He watched the clock as he put things away, wiping down tables and gathering bottles off surfaces to toss. Slowly but surely, people migrated toward the door.

Everyone, that was, except for the birthday crew.

"Come on, guys. It's over. Time to call it a night." He took another look at the time. It was three minutes to two.

"We're not done," one of the college, frat boy wannabes goaded. He leaned on a friend with a hiked elbow, sneering at Dean. "What are you going to— to do?" He slugged more of his beer, frowning when he hit bottom.

"Kick your asses out, that's what I'm going to do."

Dean turned with his hands full of bottles and glasses, in no mood to play games. He had the Sheriff on speed dial for nights like this. Nine-one-one was great, but he had permission to get help directly. *Then* he'd call emergency and tell them who, what, and where.

Without warning, a hard hand slammed down on his shoulder and spun him around. It happened so fast he cringed, waiting for the fist in the face.

Only it didn't happen that way.

"Fucking Christ!" was followed by a howl of pain.

"Never throw this out again. I *will* break it. Understand?"

Dean blinked, swallowing hard. The smack he heard hadn't been his face being pummeled. It had been the solid impact of flesh being caught in a palm. And held. Without shaking.

"Fuck you! Get us drinks!"

"Yeah!"

"It's Robbie's birthday! We're not leaving!"

"I think you've had enough. Dean has asked nicely for you to leave. You have two minutes or *I* will ask." The tall stud leaned close into Dean's attacker's face. "I won't be using words."

"You can't fight us all."

Dean knew the kid was right, but tall and gorgeous didn't seem to agree.

He smiled.

The man *fucking* smiled. It was the kind of smile that sent shivers down a sane man's back. Obviously, he was the only sane one left in the bar. It had cleared out fast when this started. So much for help from any regulars.

"I was hoping you'd feel that way. Dean, you heard them, right? They wanted this."

A table toppled over, crashing hard as two more advanced. They looked like jocks, broad and blunt, with acorns for brains.

"Do I have your permission to be of help?" He twisted enough to glance at Dean. "Please?" he asked kindly.

"Don't break them," he managed, joking, but fearing it was a possibility.

"I'll do my best," he replied. He faced the man at the other end of the fist he held. "Last chance."

"There's only two of you, and there's eight of us," someone slurred.

"Wrong answer."

Dean leaped out of the way when the man in leather moved with a speed that left him speechless.

He arched an arm and spun the drunk in front of him, smooth as ballet. The young idiot's chest pushed outward with his arm now jammed between his shoulder blades. He cried out in drunken shock.

"Let's take this outside, shall we?" the guy all but purred.

"Get him!"

The two jocks jumped him, shoving Dean out of their way. He flew backwards, bottles flying and glass shattering where it landed. Before they destroyed the bar, he clawed to stand, racing for the phone.

He hit the speed dial for Sheriff Archer. "Kelly, it's Dean. All hell's about to break loose."

"On my way. Call it in." The phone disconnected.

Dean called emergency and made the report.

"Excuse me, could you repeat that?"

Whatever he'd been saying had slowed to a stupefied drool. He watched as two of the partiers were caught in fists, heads clunked together like dolls, and then their limp forms were escorted for the door.

His tall savior wasn't even breathing hard.

"Are you still there?"

"Yes! Yes, still here," he croaked. "There's a… Ah, uh…" He watched in disbelief as someone took a swing that was so badly executed, a little leaguer could have been behind it.

Only the biker didn't swing back. He ducked and came up under the man's arm, cutting him off in the middle to haul him outside in a fireman's carry. Dean presumed to dump him, because he wasn't gone long.

"Mr. Eckler? Are you there?"

"Yes. I… Let me call you back. Sheriff Archer will be here to oversee things in a few minutes."

After another affirmative, he numbly hung up the phone. The guy hadn't even taken off his jacket.

Three remained, and they circled his apparent new bouncer of the evening.

"Come on, boys. You really don't want to do this," he chided them. He left them room but they still tried to find him with jabs and punches, dividing his attention.

Dean walked forward, but a raised palm made him halt with a foot in the air.

"Check on the kids outside. I have these."

"You're crazy," Dean rebuked him.

"You're outnumbered, assface," one of the jocks jeered. "You're gonna need his help."

"Don't think so," he replied, indifferent to their taunts.

Dean watched them cautiously as he edged in front of the bar. He was about halfway to the door when his feet froze and his jaw dropped open.

One of the jocks took a swing and another tried to jump on the guy's broad back. It looked like a timed effort they'd used before. This time it didn't work. A single motion had the clinging monkey flying to smack into the third, leaving the one who tried to hit him as the last man standing. A *come and get me* hand curl was like fanning a red banner in front of a bull.

He charged.

And was laid out cold with a single punch.

"Holy shit! Is he alive?"

A dry snort was his answer. "I hear the Sheriff outside. I'll bring these three." He stooped and hefted one over his shoulder and grasped another who wasn't unconscious by his collar. "On your feet," he growled.

Shaking and groggy, the boy obeyed.

"Could you get the door?" he asked, dragging the two drunk men with him.

Dean followed him outside, spotting the strobing lights from the cop car light up the parking lot.

"God almighty, Dean. What happened here?"

Kelly stared at him looking for answers. The five who'd already been escorted were heaped in a pile in the parking lot. A few moans could be heard.

"Drunk and disorderly." Two more bodies were added to the pile. "They refused to exit the premises."

"Dean?"

"He's telling the truth." Dean searched the pile of limbs and faces, pointing. "He took a swing when I refused to serve them more." He threw a look over his shoulder at the other man who'd vanished inside for the last one. "He stopped it. They tried to jump him. He's been bringing them out. I saw him physically hit only one, and it was on the defensive."

Kelly scratched at his scalp under his hat, his winter coat making a nylon rasp. "I can't cart eight college whelps to jail."

"Call their mothers." The last one slithered to the pile. The one that had been laid out cold by one punch. "It's what would have happened to me. You never wanted to call my mother with this kind of news. My ass wouldn't have found a comfortable way to sit for a week. Even at that age."

"Who are you?" Now that he was getting over his shock, Dean realized exactly how much this man had done for him tonight. He didn't look like he'd even broken a sweat.

"Cade Rose." He offered a hand. "And I didn't break any of them."

"Dean Eckler."

His hand was engulfed in hard heat. He had smooth skin, but a strong grip.

"Do you want to press charges, Dean?"

He considered it, but not for long. "They're outside now. Other than knocking over a few tables and glasses, they didn't destroy anything. Cade stopped them before it got to that." *Thank God.* He knew he'd managed to save more than the bar tonight. The rare night he worked alone. The one night he'd been at risk.

He sighed and faced Sheriff Archer, making himself focus again. "Do what you need to do to get them out of here. I have a bar to clean up. I'm not pressing charges. Make sure they understand that's a good thing."

He swung around on a heel and aimed for the heavy door, getting out of the cold. He left it unlocked in case Kelly had to talk to him. What surprised him, though, was about five minutes later, Cade followed him.

"Would you like some help?"

Dean leaned with a hip to the bar and studied the man. He seemed sincere. And after just taking on eight drunks, he had faith he wasn't there to cause Dean any harm.

"Honestly, I'd love it."

Cade nodded and slid out of his leather jacket to lay it over a stool.

Chapter Two

Cade picked up the tables that had been knocked over, making sure they were steady enough to still use. Then he stacked chairs on the ones Dean had already cleaned. Once those were up, he grabbed a broom. Dean was sweeping up glass, so he pushed stuff on the floor in his direction to be swept into a trash bin.

"Anything else you need help with?"

Dean leaned on his broom. "Nah, not really." He dipped his head, then looked up through thick lashes. "I want to thank you. You saved me and the bar tonight."

Cade rolled a shoulder. "I wish they hadn't been so drunk. Takes the fun out of it."

"Oh, you go bar busting on a regular basis?" Dean snickered.

Cade huffed with laughter. "No. Just needed to blow some steam." It hadn't cured anything, but it had helped. Gave him a few minutes to get out of his own head, anyway. Especially since Dean had specifically asked he not break anyone. He wouldn't have hurt anyone, but it had required a little deeper restraint. He wouldn't hurt someone not on the attack, unless they were already looking for a fight from him first. Even when he fought with pack, it was never to harm.

He handed off the broom. "I hope you enjoy the holiday. Got plans?"

Dean lowered his chin to rest on propped hands on the top of the held handle. "Sit at home, probably."

Cade shrugged into his coat. "Why?"

"No one to spend it with."

"Not even friends?"

Dean's green eyes closed. "Long story short, I don't have many and they're not around right now."

"So, what? Three days of staring at TV?"

"In my pajamas," he shared. "Exciting, I know."

Cade debated for about three seconds. "Busy in the morning?"

"No."

"Would you like something to do?"

"Depends."

"It involves food. Good food," Cade offered, enticingly.

"Food? Home cooked?"

Cade smiled for him. "If I know my brother-in-law, very homemade."

Dean scrubbed a palm over his chin. "Where at?"

"We could meet at my place. Silo."

Dean stood a little straighter, more attentive. "Silo? Where the bad storms were last fall?"

"Yeah."

"That's a bit of a drive for food," Dean hedged, sounding less enthusiastic.

"I know." He stuffed his hands into his pockets. "Actually, you'd be doing me a favor. Call it a trade for helping tonight. It doesn't help that I'm the last single man standing."

"Everyone's hitched?" Dean asked.

"More or less. It's not uncomfortable."

Dean leaned again. "But it is."

"Yeah," Cade agreed. "So what do you say?" He took a short step forward and froze. His nose twitched. The scent... Skin. Male.

His wolf perked up.

Cade's heart lurched.

No. Fucking. Way.

This wasn't possible. It wasn't right. It couldn't be. Not a guy. He liked women. Had *always* liked women. It was right in front of him now and his wolf was paying attention.

His wolf was wrong. *Dead wrong.*

He formed the words, thought it out to let Dean off the hook so Cade could get the hell out of there. He wasn't fast enough.

"What time?"

Cade mentally slapped himself to not let the internal confusion show. He answered the question. It was about all the capacity he had suddenly. He was in shock. This was wrong on so many levels.

And he'd started it. He was cursing a blue streak inside.

"Jamie said ten, so my place about quarter of?"

Dean seemed to think about it, then, "Okay." He rested the broom against the bar and walked around to the register. After rolling out receipt paper, he tore it in half. He wrote out his number and handed it over. "Give me yours and your address. I'll look it up in the morning for directions. You're sure they won't mind an extra person?"

"They won't mind."

Cade's fingers gripped at the paper, almost dropping the offered pen trying to avoid touching him now. He didn't know how he'd missed the nuances outside, touching him, standing close, but… *fuck*. He was so positive, he was terrified.

And he'd invited the man to eat with them. He whimpered inside. Keeping his gaze lowered, he wrote out the information.

Cade knew his wolf was wrong. He *had* to be wrong. Dean couldn't be gay, and Cade knew he wasn't. He slid the paper over wood. He was trying to be nice to a guy who sounded like he was going to be alone for the holiday. That was all.

"If you need to, just call." He didn't want to sound like he wanted him to get lost. Cade honestly hoped he didn't show, that he blew off the invite.

This time, Cade would be so grateful if he accidentally slept in.

Dean picked up the slip and put it in a pocket, then offered a hand. "Thanks."

Hiding everything, denying everything, Cade shook. "Glad tonight wasn't worse."

Dean let him go, swinging a glance around the now brightly lit, empty bar. "You and me both." Dean focused on him and smiled, a little tired, and warm. "See you for chow."

Cade nodded and casually walked away, the hand he'd shook with shoved into a pocket. It was locked tight in a fist.

His palm burned.

Once outside, he sucked a hard draught of air, shivering as the cold hit his sinuses and lungs.

The man's scent wasn't fading. He growled.

On a night when he'd needed to clear his head, blow some steam, and get his shit together, he'd instead found another headache.

Because there was no way in hell this was possible.

* * * *

Dean drove up to the curb in front of the quaint, light blue house. He yawned, drinking down the last of his cooled coffee. Waking to his alarm clock hadn't been the most welcome start of his day, but when food he wouldn't have to cook for himself was on the offering table… Yeah, that was a little harder to pass up.

Besides, he had days ahead of him he could sleep. After replacing the cup, he got out of the car. Yards were decorated with festive ornaments and standing displays. Strings of lights wrapped houses and trees. He was sure it was a festive sight after dark. The dusting of snow still on the ground would be added to in the coming days. They were anticipating a heavy fall to hit on Christmas night.

Oh, fun.

He planned on being wrapped up under quilts watching TV before it even started.

Clearing the car's bumper, he walked up to the front door and knocked. In the light of day, without the hue of bad lighting and the after-hours tiredness getting in the way, Cade was positively awe-inspiring when he opened the door.

"Hey," he said. "Come on in."

"I'm good on time?"

"Perfect."

Dean caught the slightest grumble. "Everything good?"

As he turned his back, Cade ran a hand over his head, plying through the loose length of hair draped down his back. Dean wanted to run his fingers through it. Instead, he watched as it was quickly grabbed and tied it off with an elastic band.

"Yeah. Need my jacket."

Dean stole a quick glimpse around the room when Cade vanished around the corner. Maybe he didn't wake up the most sociable type of person. He wouldn't be the first.

He reappeared shrugging into a wool-lined Sherpa coat.

"No leather this morning, huh?" he joked.

Cade tugged at the bottom. "Heh, no. No motorcycles this morning."

Dean noticed he was wearing sneakers this morning too. Didn't matter. He was still gorgeous. He kept his raunchy fantasies quiet, locked up tight with a titanium mental key.

Cade plucked a key ring off a hook near the door. Dean left first when he opened it. Cade locked it and then Dean followed as he veered to the left for a pickup in the driveway.

He read the door decal. "Rose Veterinary."

Cade unlocked the truck and they both hopped in. "My brothers and I run the town clinic."

"Three vets?" He buckled up. That was different.

"It gets better," he warned. He started to put the truck in reverse then froze. "Shit. Uh, bad time to mention this, but you don't have a problem with people being gay, do you?" Cade studied him, a hint of real concern ghosting over his expression.

"Nope. None." Dean smiled. *Joke's on you, friend.* "Why?" He knew Cade wasn't asking out of interest.

"You'll see."

"Should I be worried?" He frowned, wondering what Cade was driving at.

"Half the house is gay. My brother will be there with his husband. Chris' ex will have his boyfriend. The only woman will be Maya, Quade's girl."

"Wow. One woman. She must feel special."

Cade snickered. "If she's noticed, she doesn't play on it." He slowed at a stop sign and then turned out to the main road, driving down Main Street the way Dean had arrived.

"Which are your brothers?"

"Quade and Chris. Ed is Chris' ex. Good guy. Firefighter here in town."

"And they're still friends?"

"We're a small community, and those like my brother and Ed tend to stick together."

Dean guessed that was Cade's polite way of saying he *wasn't* like them. He'd assumed as much. He was scorching hot, but Dean's gaydar didn't so much as ping, much less go all systems alarm over the man.

He softened the sigh of disappointment. "Thanks for inviting me, by the way." He relaxed on the seat with his hands in his jacket pockets. The truck was warming nicely now that they were moving at a good clip.

"It's all good. No one should be home alone this time of year. Whether it's Christian or Christmas, Winter Solstice, or whatever anyone wants to call it. Besides, Jamie was begging us to be here today." He gave Dean a bashful grin that almost charmed him right across the seat. "Honestly, you *are* doing me a favor. I love them all, but being there alone…" He faced forward to drive, but Dean understood. He was outnumbered.

"It's cool. No one has to know you picked me up at a bar last night," Dean quipped.

Cade whipped around to blink at him, then busted out with laughter. "Good one. That's good." Broad shoulders rocked as he shook his head.

Dean gazed outward when Cade turned off the road. "Wow. This is your brother's place?"

"It was ours originally, my family's. Our parents are deceased."

"Oh, man. I'm sorry." Dean heard the restrained pain in that.

"It's been a while. Chris held us together until Quade and I finished veterinary school."

"He must be a hell of a brother."

"He is," Cade replied. He pulled up behind other vehicles. "Looks like we're only missing Ed. Ha. I'm not last for a change."

Dean chuckled at his grousing.

Together they walked to the front door, and Cade knocked. The door swung open, revealing a cute blond. "Hey, Cade." He raised a glance up to Dean where he shadowed Cade. The blond's smile never faltered. "Morning. Come on in."

"This is Dean. Jamie."

"Nice to meet you," Dean said, offering a hand.

"You too. Coats in the spare," Jamie instructed. Unfazed. No questions. Not so much as a blink of an eye.

Dean guessed Cade had told the truth. They really didn't mind him being there.

"That would be my old room." Cade chuckled. "Ed still coming?"

"Yep. They called about fifteen minutes ago. Chris, Quade, and Maya went to handle the horses. You know the drill." Jamie winked and hopped back to the kitchen.

"Drill?"

"Make yourself at home. They don't stand on ceremony." He tipped his head. "Let's go put the coats up and see what's on the menu."

Whatever it was smelled incredible. Savory, sweet, and homemade, the scents filled the house. Couldn't be beat. Dean tagged along, slipping out of his jacket to put it with Cade's.

"He's nice."

"He's bonkers, but he's family," Cade corrected, grinning.

Dean chuckled quietly, following him out of the room for the kitchen.

"There's coffee if you want it, or if you're like those of us who don't like mornings: coffee first, breathing second."

"That sounds great."

Cade handed him a cup and moved out of the way to let him reach the pot. It smelled divine.

"Addict ingredients are over there." Jamie pointed down the counter.

"Jamie," Cade warned.

"What?" he replied with an innocent drawl. "You never want to get between a person and their coffee. Trust me. Why do you think I'm missing fingers?"

He held up his hand, all but the middle finger curled under.

Dean covered his mouth to not snort his drink.

"Brat."

"Never said I wasn't," he countered, completely unconcerned.

"Where is Chris?" Cade groaned. "You need your keeper."

A door opened somewhere and right after, Dean heard voices.

"Are you sure you wouldn't mind?" A woman was talking.

"It's not a problem. We used to have riding horses but never replaced the geldings when they passed."

A trio entered the kitchen. A redhead, a fit and handsome guy, and... Dean gulped, then coughed. Hard. A towel was thrust at him and he covered his mouth as he gagged and coughed his way through the fit. "So... sorry," he gasped, panting to clear his passage.

"You okay?"

Dean nodded, blinking away moisture. "Plumbing problems," he croaked. He finally caught his breath and met the man's eyes to sweep back to Cade. "You're twins."

"Yeah," Cade offered, confused.

Dean gathered his thoughts, closed his eyes and drew a breath. "I wasn't expecting it." It made him think of Daniel. And doing that would put him in a mood no one wanted to suffer. Wiping his thoughts clean of his past, he found a smile and put it on display. "Sorry about that." He offered a hand. "I'm Dean Eckler."

"Nice to meet you. I'm Quade and this Maya."

He repeated it for Chris.

"Great first impression," he muttered, gripping his mug again.

Someone knocked. Quade went to answer it. Cade moved to the side of the kitchen and Dean followed. "Sorry about that."

"What happened?"

Dean could tell by Cade's expression he'd really screwed up. Seriously, it wasn't like they had three eyes. He stared into the brown liquid in his mug. "My twin died six years ago. His name was Daniel."

"Damn. I'm sorry." Cade glanced toward the front room when voices drifted toward them. "So it wasn't because I'm a twin, but it brought up memories?"

Dean nodded. "The bar was ours."

"Gemini's? It's not your birthday or whatever?"

Dean huffed mirthlessly. "No. We were exact copies. I imagine much like you two. Only we excelled in duplication." He managed a weak grin, burying it behind his mug. He did have good memories. It was the bad ones he despised.

"And I hated being an exact copy," Cade mused.

"Hey, guy." A broad guy came up to Cade and jabbed his shoulder with a fist. "Feeling better this morning?"

Cade shrugged, crossing his arms. "Wasn't feeling bad last night."

"Could've fooled me." He let it drop without a lot of pushing.

"Where's Margo? Come here, girl."

Dean watched as a dog trotted up to Jamie. He knelt to the floor and roughed her playfully, getting dog kisses in retaliation.

"Where'd she come from?"

"She's Duncan's." At the sound of his name, a guy watching the pair on the floor lifted his head and sauntered over.

Cade introduced him.

"How'd you get roped into this insanity?" Duncan leaned enough to touch shoulders with Ed.

Marked. Yeah, he got it. Dean ignored it. This morning he was only a guy sharing a little get-together time. A friend. He spared a look to Cade. At least, he guessed that's what this morning was all about. "I had some trouble at closing time last night. Cade helped me out."

"He said he was going to be at home for the next three days, watching TV. Alone."

"Why do that when we have this?" Ed motioned over his head, getting a scoffing laugh from people.

"You're only here because you want the rest of the ham, Ed. Don't think I don't know that," Jamie pointed out good-naturedly.

"Busted!" Maya cried.

Ed arched an eyebrow at her where she snuggled up against Quade's front. She stuck her tongue out at him. She knew she was safe.

He faced Duncan. "And *that* is why I'm gay."

"Butthead."

"Gee, she does fit in, doesn't she?" Cade shot to his brother, snickering wholeheartedly.

"If we ever played football, it wouldn't be shirts and skins. It would be smartasses and the *men*." Ed grinned right at the fiery redhead.

"Okay, now wait a minute." Jamie stood, scowling. "Which team would that put me on?"

Chris encircled him from behind around the waist. "Baby, if you have to ask," he teased.

Maya started giggling behind her hand.

"Just you wait, fur ball," Jamie groused, but not too threateningly. It was pretty clear Chris would never hurt a hair on Jamie's head.

"Are we getting fed this morning or what?" Quade asked.

"Yeah, yeah." Jamie sighed and Chris let him go. "Set the table. It's ready."

"Your wish," Chris said, not terribly loud, but Dean caught it. It came across like a sensual caress.

Dean bit his lip. Damn, being alone sucked. Being lonely in a room full of people, especially when one of those people really turned him on and was utterly off limits, sucked the hardest.

Chapter Three

Cade was fighting his wolf's insistence. Since he'd opened the door to the man, his wolf had been pacing inside, determined and almost aggressive with his adamancy. All Cade knew was it was wrong. He was being a friend. Dean was not his mate.

He couldn't be.

"Oh, man. This is good."

Cade peeked to his side. Dean was in epicurean heaven. His eyelids hovered half-closed, slowly enjoying what he was eating. The sheer pleasure on his features said everything.

"The ham?" Ed asked.

"Mm hm," he replied, too engrossed to actually speak.

Ed smiled smugly. Cade spotted Jamie's satisfied pleasure accompanied by a light blush on his face.

"Thanks, guys."

"What did you do to it?"

"What? And give away my secret?" he said mysteriously, ruining it by laughing. "It's actually something simple. I injected it."

"With what? Pork crack?" Ed stuck a thick slice on a biscuit and tore into it. "I'm addicted."

"It's a broth injection. The details will go to the grave with me."

"Damn." Maya sighed. "Can't I bribe you? This beats my Nana's and that's hard to do."

Dean shifted on his chair following conversation and his leg brushed Cade's under the table. Cade swallowed abruptly at the contact, the food on his tongue becoming a sudden lump. It went down feeling like a rock as it hit his stomach. Heat flashed and burned. He knew it was innocent. They were side by side. It wasn't like he was playing with Cade under the table. Tremors shook his frame with the force of a small electrical current. He had to move. Suddenly he had to get away.

"Excuse me?" He jerkily stood and rushed from the room. Unsure where to go, he blindly opened the rear door. Once outside, he fell to the side of the house against his back, sucking hard breaths to clear his senses. The man's scent was infiltrating his pores. He scrubbed his hands over his face, clawing with mental fingernails to find his balance.

He was failing so badly, it wasn't funny.

"Hey, you okay?" Chris stood holding the door, watching with clear worry. "You hurt Jamie."

"What?" The rush of his heart was making his ears ring.

"Running out like that. He's been working for days for last night and this morning."

"No. No, no. It's… It's not him. Not the food." *Fuck.* He covered his face. "I'm okay. Just…give me a minute."

Chris studied him, doubtful. "If you want to talk about something, you know Quade and I are here for you."

Cade nodded, staring at the tips of his shoes, at nothing. "Yeah." He shoved his fingers into his jeans pockets. He'd forgotten it was freezing out there. "I'll be there in a minute."

Chris waited for a drawn out moment then, thankfully, went inside without demanding explanations. He knew he didn't have one to give. Cade knew he was being an ass. There was no reason for him to act this way. He didn't know how to explain it. How to describe the heat. The need... He groaned, his head resting with a dull thud against the outer wood. Yes. *Need.* He had no idea what it was or what to do about any of it. He'd never even kissed a man. He repeated the cranial thwacks against the side of the house. He didn't know how to deal with this, or his wolf.

So he ran.

It wasn't like Dean was throwing himself at him. For all he knew, the man was straight. Accepting, but straight. He hadn't given any signs otherwise. His breath left him to make a blustery cloud on a harsh exhale.

This was so wrong. He liked Dean. As a friend. *Only* as a friend.

The door opened. Expecting Chris again, or Jamie, he couldn't have been more surprised to see Dean.

"Look, if my being here is that much of an issue—"

"Fuck." It was a growl. "It's not— They all like you." It would have been so much easier if they hadn't.

Dean closed the door to stand with him, to talk privately. "You don't."

Cade felt two feet tall hearing the man say that. He'd never wanted to make him think he wasn't welcome, wasn't liked. Dean seemed to be a great guy. But he was still a *guy*. Cade was fighting against his wolf, horns locked liked two bulls, when there was no question. Not to his mind.

"I don't know why you invited me if you can't stand me."

Cade raked a hand through his hair, hitting the band and tugging against it. "I'm sorry. I swear..." He cleared his throat when it tightened, making him sound raw. "You're fine. It's me."

"Prove it. I almost didn't come because you gave this same vibe last night right before you left. I'm not stupid. You regretted it for some reason as soon as you offered. So let's cut through the bullshit. Get your insane ass back in here and finish." He sighed. "Then we'll leave and you'll never see me again."

With that parting message, he opened the door and went inside. Where it was warm. Where his brothers were probably wondering what had crawled up his ass this morning.

Ed thought he'd been messed up last night.

Last night had nothing on today.

He had to get through his morning. He would drive Dean to his car and that would be the end of it. He'd never see the man again.

The echoing howl that decision produced almost drove him to his knees. He clutched his head. "No," he snapped. "You are wrong."

Battling his instincts and his wolf back into the shadows, he finally began to feel marginally in control again. He wiped a hand over his face, feeling the sheer cold on his skin. It bit at him, sharp and insistent.

Clouds of ice formed on the air with each panted breath. He shoved off the wall and reached for the doorknob. He didn't want to ruin the morning for anyone. Jamie had worked his ass off to see last night's Christmas party a success. This morning was about family.

It was time he acted like he was a part of it.

He walked up behind Jamie's chair and leaned close enough to kiss his cheek. "I'm sorry, baby bro."

Jamie wrapped a hand upward to curl over his head. "It's okay. Go finish up." He nudged Cade to take his seat.

Next to Dean.

He nodded to Dean as he did, glancing around the table. "It's all good. Something I had to deal with."

Those at the table who knew, would suspect his wolf, but they would be so far off the mark guessing *what* had agitated the beast. The question in Dean's gaze was the one that killed him.

No. Cade didn't dislike him. Didn't hate the man. Dean's opinion was so wrong, it was almost laughable.

He knew he should say something, but he couldn't, and not in front of a dozen eyes. Hopefully, he'd be able to find the right words by the time they were leaving, because it wasn't that long of a drive from Chris' to Cade's to try to correct the problems he was creating.

* * * *

Dean relaxed on his chair, stuffed to his eyeballs. He sipped on his coffee. "This was amazing. If this was some part of what you had last night, I'm jealous." He'd had a cold burger for dinner.

Jamie ticked off items on his fingers. "There was the ham sliced with cheese and crackers, sandwiches, bacon bombs, fruit slices and dips."

"Fudge and cookies," Maya offered.

"And don't forget the cider." Ed drained his mug with an appreciative slurp.

"Stop!" Dean held up a hand, laughing. "You're killing me."

"What happened last night? You said Cade helped you out." Chris pushed his cleaned plate forward.

"I own a bar in Cassan, Gemini's. A birthday crowd showed up about ten thirty and refused to leave at close."

"So Cade growled at them, right?" Jamie teased, ducking when Cade tossed a bread crust at him. He pressed into Chris' shoulder, making a *missed me* face in Cade's direction.

"No. One of them tried to start a fight, and Cade shut it down. By the time Sheriff Archer arrived, he had all but three out in the parking lot. We straightened up the mess they'd made in trying to cause the fight, and then he asked me to come here this morning."

"We're glad nothing serious happened," Maya said with a generous smile.

"Any friend of Cade's is welcome here," Chris interjected.

Dean nodded, knowing it was the polite thing to say. He wasn't disillusioned enough to think he was really a friend. Cade had made it perfectly clear. He should have paid better attention and heeded the warning signs when he saw them last night, rather than doubt his own tired judgment.

"I appreciate that," he replied, keeping to the script. "I have to admit, you've got a good family here." That he did mean. He studied the table. "Brothers, friends, husbands, and girlfriends. Well, one girlfriend," he amended, tipping his head toward Maya. "How do you put up with all of them?"

She batted her lashes. "Practice. Lots and lots of practice."

Snickers and guffaws circled the table.

She squealed when Quade goosed her. At least he guessed that was what made her bounce like a rabbit on her chair.

He wasn't sure what was next, but there was definitely a laid back air to the morning.

"Cade, why don't you give Dean the tour?" That was Chris.

Cade sat a little straighter. "Oh, um. Sure." He faced Dean at the table. "Want to? You can meet the horses."

"Sure."

"Go ahead," Chris nudged, sharing a look with Cade that Dean couldn't decipher. "We'll clean up. Fresh coffee and cider when you come in should hit the spot."

Dean tipped his mug, getting the last drops. "If there's more of this, I'll do anything."

"Anything?" Ed mused, rubbing his chin with pure contemplative villainy.

Dean quickly lifted his hands. "Okay, maybe not quite *anything*."

"Nice save," Duncan murmured, humor coloring his words.

"C'mon." Cade tapped his shoulder. "We better run while the getting is good. I'll grab our coats."

Dean waited for him to return, buttoning up before he popped open the refrigerator to grab a few carrots. He followed through the rear door, both sauntering for the barn. Heavy clouds were building.

It looked like the threat of Christmas snow was going to become a reality.

"In case you were wondering, that was my brother's way of telling me to apologize."

Dean walked at Cade's shoulder. He knew Cade was a little taller, but now in sneakers, it wasn't as much as he'd originally thought. "Apologize for what?" He curled fingers into fists in his pockets to keep them warm.

"For being an ass."

"We all have those days."

Cade opened the side door. "Yeah, but you didn't do anything to deserve it."

It was warmer in the barn. The scents of hay, grain, dust, and horse were thick in the air.

"So why ask me to come if you don't like me?" Dean figured he had a right to know.

"It's not that." Cade grumbled, snapping the carrots in half as they cleared the barn. "I've been dealing with a lot of shit recently."

"Oh?"

Cade walked up to a stall where a monster black horse lazily watched them. He started feeding the behemoth the carrot halves. "This is Tiberius, or Bear. He's Chris' wagon horse. The kids love him."

"And the little guy?" A pert nose was pushing against the gate next to Bear's stall.

"Biscuit. They're best buds. Biscuit was a rescue. Chris took him in and he's been here since."

Dean scratched between Biscuit's ears. Cade had slid right past his curiosity, so he expected for him to continue to ignore it. Cade surprised him when he didn't.

"I don't know how to explain it."

"So try," Dean offered, keeping his focus on horse mane and ears to not add pressure to the man at his side.

"Chris has Jamie. Quade met Maya."

Dean understood. At least he thought this could be the problem. Cade had said he was the last man standing, so to speak. "And it's making you feel like you need to hurry up and find yours."

Cade snorted and leaned on his elbows a bit, petting Tiberius. "I guess."

"Are they pressuring you?"

"No."

Dean nodded, thinking. "So why the asshole act?"

Cade's jaw worked back and forth.

"Okay, I get it. You have a gay brother. You don't want any of them thinking you're gay because you brought a male friend to breakfast. Is that it?" That irked him. Geez, the man had a gay brother, and friends. Did he really feel it was that much of an insult to be seen as gay himself?

"Chris knows I'm not."

Dean's hand faltered in its petting. Chris might know, but unless he was hearing things in the man's voice, *Cade* wasn't as sure. Now he was even more confused, trying to understand what wasn't being said, or decide if he was imagining it.

"Forget it." Cade stood straight and faced Dean. "It's not you. I do mean that. And I'm not sorry for bringing you. Or for being your friend."

"Friends?" He withheld the derisive snort. The man *had* fed him after all. Not sure how much leeway he could grant aside from that though.

"Yeah, man. We're friends." Cade gave him a smile. "It's my problem, not yours. It'll work itself out."

He patted at Biscuit again. "Tell me something."

"Shoot." He handed over a carrot so Biscuit could get some.

"Do *you* have a problem with people being gay?" Dean kindly fed the patient animal. He seemed much calmer about it than the beast bumping and chomping against Cade hunting for more.

"Course not," he said. "Whoever makes you happy isn't my concern."

Dean tossed that around for a few minutes. "So it wouldn't matter to you if I was?"

"But you're not." Cade twisted to pierce him with turbulent, gray eyes. "Are you?"

"Depends. Are we still friends if I am?"

"What kind of a— Oh." Cade pulled his hands away from a nosing Bear demanding more carrots. He faced forward. "It doesn't matter to me."

Dean felt that wall go up so fast, the breeze moved his hair. Fine. He wasn't going to force anyone to like him. Wasn't going to force anyone to spend time with him, as a friend or whatever. He was sorry friendships were conditional with Cade. Especially considering his family, he really wouldn't have believed this of the man.

He sighed slowly. Never fails. Scorching hot and utterly unattainable. Not even as a friend. Why should Cade be any different from everyone else he'd known? Times like this made him miss Daniel that much more. Danny never would have left him, never would have turned his back on him.

"Ready for something hot?"

Dean patted Bear's broad face and scratched Biscuit's ear. "Yeah. I guess so." *Then you can take me home.*

He knew he'd never see Cade again. He may say one thing but his eyes, and everything else, said something completely different.

Chapter Four

Cade helped Chris pitch hay down from the loft a week later. Christmas had come and gone. Snow a foot and a half thick covered the ground. Old Man Winter had officially moved in.

He'd spent a little longer with Chris and the gang on Christmas Eve morning, then had driven home so Dean could pick up his car. They'd said their goodbyes and he'd left.

Cade hadn't driven to Cassan, hadn't been to Gemini's, and hadn't made any efforts to call the man.

It was Quade's week at the clinic, which meant Cade had the overnight short straw anyway. He didn't have the *freedom* to drive to Cassan.

At least that was what he told himself. So there hadn't been any after-hours emergencies fielded by the clinic. Didn't matter. He had to be there.

"Cade!"

He looked down over the edge, yelling down to his brother. "Yeah?"

"That's enough. We're good."

He spotted the stack against the wall. He'd lost track. "Okay." Instead of taking the ladder, he jumped, landing in a crouch. "Got it all where you want it?" he asked when he stood.

Chris nodded in answer. "Jamie wanted me to ask if you wanted to come by and watch the ball drop tonight. Quade passed. Maya came down with a flu, so he's keeping up with her at home."

"That sucks. She's okay, though?" He tugged off his gloves, and shoved the pair into a rear pocket.

"Yeah, just miserable."

That was one good thing to be said about having lupine blood. They never got sick. "Anyone else?"

"Just friends."

"The usual suspects?" he joked. "Sure. I'm not going out anywhere on call. You don't get tired of Jamie doing this all the time?"

"What? Making us a family?" Chris jabbed Cade with a sharp elbow. "I love him for it. We need this. All of us. Just because I'm mated doesn't mean we stop being a family."

"We do stuff, all three of us."

"Running once a month doesn't count. But that's only us, too." Chris sat on a bale of hay. "This is something more. It's something he needs, too. A way to be needed and feel like he belongs. He can't shift, but he can be with the pack on his terms. This is one of those ways that helps him."

"Huh." Cade plopped down on a bale next to him. "I never really thought of it that way." It did make sense, though.

"He doesn't talk about his dad much."

"Can you blame him?" Cade pointed out. "He was a bastard."

Chris snorted and crossed his arms. "Don't have to tell me. I think this helps him because of the way his dad treated him. He likes having people here. And so long as they don't move in, I do too."

Cade punched Chris' shoulder affectionately. "Turning into the old married couple already."

"Shut up." He was grinning though. "So, put you down for one or two?"

"Just one."

Chris gave him a confused stare. "Where's Dean?"

Cade looked away, because something in the far corner was suddenly *that* interesting. "I'm sure he's working tonight. New Year's at the bar."

"He was a nice guy."

Cade didn't reply. He wasn't going to argue that. It was true.

"Is he single?"

Cade nodded. At least, he guessed Dean was. He hadn't made any boyfriend noises in the time they'd spent together. Cade knew Dean and Jamie had talked some before they'd left. Maybe Jamie was going to find him a date. He tried to not let the thought… Too late. He absolutely hated it.

He had to quit this. Cade lurched from the hay. "I better go check on things and clean up. What time?"

"Anytime after nine." Chris walked beside him out of the barn. "We'll have snacks and stuff."

"Okay. I'll see you then."

He knew Chris was watching him walk away. He felt the weight of his stare the entire way.

It didn't matter what his brother thought. Dean was a friend. Nothing more. It didn't matter what his wolf thought, because it was wrong. Dead wrong.

* * * *

Dean's breath rushed in panted bursts, his chest aching. It felt like he'd been hit with a wrecking ball. He couldn't catch his breath, staring at the aftermath before him. He would have been crying, but he was

40

still too angry. Fury boiled in his veins. The impact of the loss hadn't hit yet. It would.

Gemini's was gone.

He'd received a phone call at four thirty-nine, right after he'd gone to bed. The security company had reported a tripped alarm. The police had been notified. As he was getting dressed, he received another call.

"Dean, this is Sheriff Archer."

"I'm on my way, Kelly. Have to find my shoe." He dug a sneaker out from under the bed where he'd kicked it, keeping the phone pinned between his ear and shoulder. He hopped around, one thought on his mind. To get to the bar and clear the alarm.

"You need to sit down."

Something in Kelly's voice registered, and it knifed him with a dread coldness. "What?"

"It was more than the alarm."

"Kelly," he growled, short on temper.

"The fire department is trying to save it."

"Fuck!" He disconnected the call and rushed to find suitable clothing to be outside, then snatched his jacket off the wall as he flew out the front door.

Now he stood with his jacket hanging open, his sneakers untied, and his jaw pinched so tight, his teeth ached.

The fire crew was wrapping up hose. They'd done what they could, but the age of the building had been a factor, all wood, from floor to ceiling. And all the liquor. It was like setting fire to kerosene stored in a box of kindling.

"The alarm company said something tripped the perimeter alarm and then set off the sprinkler system. There was a fifteen minute interval after the perimeter alarm tripped to first responder contact." He flipped a little spiral notepad. "Their report is the sprinkler system kicked in before responder contact."

Dean hadn't been able to look away from the smoldering mess. "What does that mean?"

"It means someone went inside and intentionally started it."

Dean blinked, tiredness and cold playing against him, making him groggy and any thinking difficult. "Run that by me again."

"It's my opinion someone torched it."

"Wait. Why did it take fifteen minutes for someone to alert you guys about the alarm?" He was sure it took several minutes for either the Sheriff or the fire department to reach Gemini's after those phone calls.

"I don't know. You need to take that up with the alarm company. I'm only giving you the timetable they gave me."

"So what you're saying is the alarm company let whoever broke in have fifteen minutes to do whatever, and then you guys were called." And by then, the place could have been in full blaze. By the sight before him, he didn't doubt it had been.

"You'll want to confirm that report for insurance." He tapped the notebook. "I'll keep this handy in case you need a second statement for evidence."

"You do that." Dean was going to hang someone's ass out to dry over this. "When can the investigator look?"

"I really doubt it'll be today, if he's even in the area."

Dean pushed a flat palm down his face, hard. "Can it be secured so no one tries to mess with anything?"

"Not today. I'll put tape around it, but that's all I can do for now. I have three on-duty officers for the next twenty-four hours. If people knew how slim we really are, there'd be hell to pay."

"Because of the holiday."

"Because of the holiday," Kelly agreed. "It's not like you're surrounded by businesses that are going to stir curiosity to check it out."

Dean looked in either direction. They were a half mile from the next intersection and about two miles out of Cassan itself. It wasn't heavily populated, a few wide lot subdivisions, mostly grounded trailers with the random site-built home. An unused lot was behind him, also a storage yard for one of the electrical contract companies, and the empty business offices, closed for the holiday. That was it in just about every direction. The closest gas station was a mile away.

Whoever had done this had no problem getting to the rear where the delivery door was and getting in unseen, doing their worst, then sneaking away before anyone showed. Hell, thanks to his so-called security company, the prick had *plenty* of time.

Dean scrubbed his face again.

"I need the investigator to contact me as soon as he's available. I'll be on the phone with the alarm company management as soon as I find whose ass I need to chew out." He'd get the printed time reports first, *then* rip someone a new asshole. *Fifteen fucking minutes!* He wanted to scream. Fifteen minutes from break-in to emergency contact. His stomach rolled like he was going to be sick. He swallowed several times, holding it all back. Everything he had in the world — gone.

Kelly wrote up the damage and call reports, giving Dean a copy. He folded them and shoved the pages into a coat pocket. He'd need those for the insurance. He ground his teeth the entire time.

When Kelly turned off his strobe lights, Dean knew he was heading out. Dean leaned against the fender of his car, staring at the trails of smoke that seeped from the wood. Steam hovered like a fog in the cold over the wood now that temperatures were infiltrating. It would ice over in a few hours if the temps held. Snow stood on either side of the building, marked, gutted, and slashed with soot from the fire. The parking lot had been scraped by the local road plow. Nothing had been left pristine after the fire and the vehicles had done their damage. The building hadn't collapsed. The frame had held up well, but he didn't have to see the inside to know it was officially destroyed. Thousands of dollars in liquor, gone.

Fishing for the reports, making sure he had them, he bumped his cell phone with his fingers. He forgot to check it before bed last night. Not that he expected anyone — Cade? — to call, but he still looked.

The message icon stuck out.

Wishful thinking was dashed when he realized it wasn't Cade.

Hope you had a good NYE. Were doing bfast if UR up for it. J.

He huffed. Up was a matter of definition.

As for his New Year's? It hadn't been all that bad. Until this. He messaged back. *I'm up early. Call me in the AM for time.*

Hell, it wasn't like he had anything else to do. Now. Or anytime in the near future.

He was in the bathroom shaving when the cell phone tones went off. Grabbing a towel to wipe his face, he loped into the living room where his coat was and sought his phone in his pocket.

"Hey, Jamie."

"Morning. What time did you get my message?"

"After six this morning, I guess."

"Did you party all night?" he teased.

Dean groaned, padding to the bedroom to finish getting properly dressed. "No, haven't been to sleep yet."

"Why not?" He heard clinks and dings in the background. Jamie was already in the kitchen.

"The bar burned down this morning."

Clank!

"Fuck!"

"Jamie?" Chris' voice echoed through the phone.

"I'm fine. Dropped the bowl," he called out. "Son of a bitch. What happened?"

"Sheriff Archer thinks arson, and I agree." Too many things left hanging in the wind, as far as he was concerned. "I'm waiting for the arson investigator, who probably won't be around until tomorrow."

"If it's the guy who helped Chris at the vet clinic, he's good. He won't skimp on the detail."

"What happened out there?"

"Come to breakfast and we'll tell you all about it."

"Sneaky."

"Yep."

Dean grinned in spite of his morning. "Coffee?"

"I'll make it strong if you haven't slept."

"Thanks." He stretched a stiff back. Tension wasn't his friend today. "Okay, yeah. What time?"

"Now. It'll be close when you get here."

"Are you that bossy with Chris?"

"Worse," he replied with a chuckle.

"Poor man. Okay. I'm on the road in ten."

"Sounds good."

Dean disconnected.

It didn't hit him until he was nearly done dressing. Jamie hadn't once mentioned Cade. Maybe Jamie and Chris could be friends regardless of what Cade did, or how he thought.

It wasn't like Dean could control who he was attracted to, like he could help the appreciation of another man's looks, or body, or hair, or eyes, or... He groaned, reprimanding himself soundly. The man had made no bones about it. Cade was straight.

Except right now Dean could really use a few friends. Once the exhaustion kicked in, he was going to be a wreck. Anger simmered, but it was one of those lying in wait angers. One he couldn't stop or feed until some kind of steps had been taken.

That involved raking the alarm company management over coals. He paid good money for that service, and they'd utterly failed at their one job. Protecting his livelihood.

For now, that anger was keeping him going. He'd crash hard soon, but right now, he was clinging onto his anger. It was really the only thing holding him up and keeping him on his feet. There was dealing with the alarm company, then insurance, then rebuilding. He was floating in a mental limbo, that frame of mind where he knew what had to be done, knew the next step, but because of the holiday, nearly everything was shut down, running with a skeleton crew if they were running at all.

He was about ten minutes from Chris and Jamie's when his cell went off.

He didn't look at the screen, guessing it would be Jamie again. He could've been knocked out by a feather when it wasn't.

"Hey, Jamie just told us. Man, I am sorry. Was anyone hurt?"

Getting over the surprise of hearing from Cade directly, he replied, "No. It started a little after four this morning. I have the deposit, small mercies, but we locked up about three forty-five, I guess. The place was a wreck after the celebrations." He read road signs as they flew past. "I'm at my turn. I'll be there in a couple of minutes."

He ended the conversation with Cade, stunned that he'd not only called, but that he'd heard actual concern in his voice.

The only vehicle he saw strolling from his car was Cade's when he arrived. Packed snow crunched under his feet. He stomped them on a step then reached for the door to knock.

When the door opened, Cade stood there. "Hey. Were the roads okay?"

"Yeah, they're all cleared now."

"That's good."

Inane chatter. Dean refused to let Cade get to him. "Who else is coming?" He stripped off his coat.

"Just us. Maya's got the flu so Quade is staying home."

She had Dean's sympathies. He hated being sick himself. But he didn't know anyone who *liked* being sick. The door closed and he realized that meant it was only *them.*

Well, he was there at Jamie's request. Not Cade's. So whatever the man thought, Dean really didn't care.

"Same place?" He jiggled the jacket in his hand.

"First door."

Dean nodded. "Morning Jamie." He paused while passing the kitchen.

"Hi!" Jamie waved with a spatula, pancakes the size of hubcaps on the flattop grill. A large dome covered a plate at his side. It looked like he'd been stacking for a while.

"Where's Chris?"

"Ran to the clinic to do the AM feedings and walks. He'll be back any minute."

Dean nodded, turning to go drop his coat in the spare on the bed. In the kitchen, he made a beeline for the coffee. "So, do you like doing all this cooking stuff?" He sipped, leaning against the counter, wondering where Cade had vanished off to. He pushed the man out of his thoughts. He didn't matter to why he was there this morning.

"Sort of. I work at the clinic as an animal tech. I don't think I want to do what the boys do. I'm not keen on bloody body parts, if you know what I mean." He grimaced.

"Unfortunately."

"I've been enjoying the holidays, because I get to play with ideas and try things, and nothing really beats food to know if you have a winner or not."

"So what are you thinking?"

Jamie flipped three cakes in a row. "I'm not sure I'm cut out for the higher volume of being a chef, or even a cook."

"What if you learned for yourself? You can do cooking as a hobby."

"I'd have to drive to Stiller Springs to attend the community college there."

Dean sipped at the hot brew in his mug. "So, is that an excuse to not do it, or an obstacle that needs to be considered? Aren't there instructional classes and videos online, too?"

Jamie huffed and glared over his shoulder. "You sound just like Chris."

Dean hid his smiles behind his drink. "I have a feeling if it's something you want to do, even if you only want to know for yourself, personally, then he'd support you. He'd help you find a way to do it."

"Damn. You nailed him completely." He stacked the finished cakes on a plate and returned the domed cover, keeping them warm. He poured out a row of three more on the griddle.

"If it's not something you want to do as a career, then you'd be learning for yourself. There's no stress in that."

"I'm not a woman," he groused.

"And only women know how to cook? I'm sure all those big names on the cooking channels would be surprised to hear that." He smirked when Jamie glared at him. "If you like it, learn it, enjoy it." He stared at his coffee. "There will come a time when your chance will be gone, or taken away from you."

He caught the wave of pain and guilt before it started beating at him. He studied his mug, avoiding Jamie's questioning glance. He wasn't ready to answer a ton of questions about this morning. It hurt like hell to see Gemini's gone, but it hurt deeper, cut in ways that he couldn't explain, how he'd also lost his last tie to his brother this morning.

The front door opened and Chris sauntered in, taking his coat off. "Mrs. Pierson's beagle misses you. I swear she cried when she saw me."

Jamie laughed, his expression lightening. "She's a good girl."

"No, she's a spoiled girl. Must be why you two understand each other."

Chris jumped out of the way when Jamie swatted at his behind with the flat of the spatula. "Smells great." He faced Dean and offered a hand. "Sorry about Gemini's. Was it an accident?"

"No. Someone triggered the alarm and delays from both the alarm company and the Sheriff doomed the building."

"Damn. I have the arson investigator's card in a file. Remind me and I'll grab it before you leave."

"That's appreciated."

The back door opened and thudded quietly shut, Cade appearing right after.

Chris went to put up his coat, Cade doing the same.

Chris set the table as Jamie started pulling pans filled with cooked sausage and scrambled eggs out of the oven. Dean's mouth watered. And for a few heartbeats, he was utterly envious of Chris.

Chapter Five

Cade was going crazy having the man so close. They weren't touching with more room at the table with only the four of them this morning. It really didn't matter. He couldn't stop staring.

Dean's hands were tanned, his nails clean and cut square. He knew without looking that his eyes were green; a mixture of green and gray, but very green. Finger-length, not quite jet-black hair. He was nearly as tall as Cade, too. Not as broad in the shoulders, but clearly fit. He'd seen what he looked like in a tight T-shirt that first night at Gemini's.

And why the fuck did all of that suddenly make his wolf go crazy? He stabbed at food on his plate. He liked women. It wasn't his fault he hadn't found one in a long time that turned him on. It wasn't his fault that he couldn't find any that attracted him, physically. His wolf didn't have to connect with every single person he met!

Apparently, he'd connected with Dean. Full-on, no holds-barred. *Mate.*

He ground his jaw.

And Chris was giving him that stare again.

"What did I do now?" he asked in exasperation.

"You're growling."

Cade started, sitting straight. "Oh… Uh. Sorry." He lowered his chin. Chris was going to take his head off for that. He hadn't been aware.

"I really appreciate the invite," Dean was saying. "But…" He stared at Cade, something sad and pitying in his gaze that sliced Cade in half. "It's pretty clear to me that Cade has issue with my being here."

"Dean—"

He shook his head, silencing Jamie. "I don't know why being gay, being friends with *your* gay brother is such a problem for you," he said right to Cade. "You're hot and cold, a friend, then an utter ass, and honestly, I don't have time or brain power to deal with you. I came as Jamie's guest this morning, not yours."

He turned on his seat and started eating again. Completely dismissing Cade.

Cade opened his mouth to apologize, but Chris' quiet snarl froze him solid.

Shit. Yeah, he was going to get it.

Chris stood from the table. "Let me see if I can find that business card. Excuse me."

Cade saw him go. He wanted to roll under the table. Chris was a loving brother, but shit, Cade was acting like an ass towards Chris' guest. Yeah, that wasn't going to win him any brotherly love.

"Be right back." He followed Chris, knowing it was exactly what Chris expected.

He closed the office door behind him, watching Chris flip through files in a cabinet drawer.

"Want to explain that to me?" Chris asked without looking up.

"Want to? No."

"Since when has being gay *ever* been an issue in this household?" The suppressed fury iced Chris' voice.

"Never!" Cade barked under his breath, keeping their argument quiet. Hearing Chris' pain stung. He'd caused that.

Chris smacked the drawer closed, the hunted for card in his fingers. "Then start talking."

Cade sagged against the closed door, his eyes closing in denial. "I'm not gay."

"What's that got to do—" The snap of the question died, the scowl leaving his brow as realization spread over his features. "You can't fight the wolf. They *do* know. As far as I know, they're never wrong, either." Silence lengthened. "Have you ever thought of a man, sexually?"

He shook his head hard.

"Why not? Even curiosity happens."

"Quade and I—"

Chris held up his hand. "Stop. Right there. You are two different people. Always have been. Always will be. Do you still find women attractive?"

He wanted to say yes so badly, but lying wouldn't do anything but add to the confusion he felt. "No," he croaked.

"How long ago was your last...?" Chris didn't finish it. Cade was grateful for that, at least. Whether it was girlfriend or screw, Cade didn't need it spelled out for him.

"Two years. I thought it was me. I thought she was right around the corner and the wolf was telling me to back off Laura. He's been deader than wood until..." He tipped his head in the general direction of the kitchen.

"And now he's all wood, huh?"

Cade snorted. "Crude, bro."

"But it's the truth, isn't it?"

Cade nodded without adding to it.

"All this fighting you're doing is going to drive him away. He thinks you hate him. Even I can see that."

"But—"

"Do you like him? In any way?"

"He's a friend."

Chris let out a breath, patience smoothing the pinched lines around his mouth. "Then start there. So he's a guy. It's not the end of the world."

"I want kids," he choked out, imploring through the pain. "I want a son. I can't be gay! How do I have kids if I'm with…" He tossed a hand angrily. "Him?"

Wide gray eyes filled his vision. "Is that… Cade?" Chris cupped his shoulder. "You've been in denial your whole life?"

Cade covered his face with spread palms. His world was falling apart. He had no idea anymore. Was it denial? He wanted to claw out his eyeballs with frustration. *He didn't know!* "What am I going to do?"

Chris gathered him against his chest. "Give nature a chance. You may get more than you could ever dream of." He ran fingers over Cade's scalp, brushing through his hair. "I know I did."

"But—"

Chris rocked him. "No. You can't use that argument. There are ways."

"I don't know how," he whispered, swallowing through a tight throat.

"Never even kissed?"

He shook his head, utterly drained. His entire life he'd known what he wanted, and how to get it. He'd gone to school, learned, and excelled. He'd known since he was in his early twenties that he wanted kids.

Making those kids required something he didn't have. He had no option but to find a woman, and he'd lived his life to see the future he wanted happen. He'd expected his mate to be female. She didn't have to be pack. It would be harder, but he knew he could do it. Chris had with Jamie. He'd never looked at men this way. A man couldn't give him what he wanted most: children. He'd never thought it would happen like this.

Now it didn't matter.

Suddenly his wolf was throwing the gauntlet and shattering all of the walls Cade had surrounding himself.

"First, you need to really apologize. Get your head on straight. He's had a shock and a half today and if you keep acting stupid, he'll never believe a word you offer from here on out."

Cade shuddered, collecting himself once more.

"Second, if he *is* a friend, then be one for him. Help him."

"You're right." Cade swallowed thickly, trying to gather his shattered soul. He had no idea how to deal with this, but it wasn't Dean's fault. Taking it out on the man was wrong, on so many levels.

"And I never, *ever,* want to hear you say anything that compares yourself to Quade, or to even me. I know you two have this little private battle going on. There is no battle. You are an awesome brother. Always have been. Quade did nothing to make you that way."

Relenting, because he needed it as much, he looped arms around Chris and squeezed. "You sound like Jamie."

"Because he's taught me what it means to speak from the heart. He's so much more than I deserve." He let Cade go. "Now, take a minute to clear your head and then we're going to help Dean with this."

Cade released a harsh exhale, the weight of the world in it. "Be right there."

Chris slipped past him through the doorway, leaving it cracked. A subtle reminder that he couldn't stay in there.

He couldn't hide, and he really needed to quit taking his issues out on Dean.

He hoped an apology would be good enough.

* * * *

Dean reached for the offered card when Chris returned. "Give this guy a call first thing in the morning. No idea when he'll get the case but establishing contact with him lets him know you're on the ball."

"Detective Gentry. Okay." He slid the card in his wallet.

"He was really detailed when we had issues last summer."

"What happened?" Dean slowly ate what was left on his plate. He'd been talking quietly with Jamie waiting for the two brothers to return. So far, only Chris was back.

"We had a drug dealer using our supply shed as a hiding place for his production paraphernalia. One of his cooking batches went bad and torched the shed." Chris motioned toward where Dean had hid the card. "He got down and dirty, found loose boards, and a dug out hole in the ground under the shed.

Between those and syringes Jamie spotted, we got fingerprints."

"He's been arrested?"

"Yes. And charged to within an inch of his life."

That was good news for Dean. The man they were describing wasn't going to cheat on anything to shortchange him. He knew there was always suspicion on owners first whenever there was insurance involved. All he wanted was to have his bar back.

The chair at his side slid quietly away from the table, distracting him.

Cade looked worn down when he scooted close to the table. He didn't know what Chris and he had discussed, but if Cade's expression was any indication, he'd been read the riot act, possibly twice.

"Have you taken any pictures?"

The question startled Dean. "Of what?"

"The bar." Cade twisted on his chair. "You're going to want pictures before they start digging around and definitely before they bring it down."

Dean's brow furrowed. He wasn't sure it was safe to be inside now. He'd have to talk to Kelly and see if he thought it was a good idea. "I'm not allowed to take anything from the building."

Cade shook his head. "You won't. But the pictures are to protect yourself. It'll be a while for the insurance to do their investigation as well. If there's any discrepancies, you'll have the oldest set of photos."

"It's already been…" He found a lit clock on the stove. "About six hours since it was reported."

"Then you should go when you're done here," Jamie suggested. "Take pictures of damaged stock, from as many angles as you can, with timestamps on everything. That's what Chris had to do to claim all the inventory we lost in the shed. The insurance company can't argue visual evidence of damaged stock."

It did sound like a good idea. If nothing else, for his own peace of mind. "I don't have a digital camera."

Cade sipped on his drink, then put it down. "If you'll let me help, I have one."

"Help?" he asked, in doubt-filled disbelief.

Cade slowly nodded. "As in, not be an ass."

Dean smirked. "Can you? Not be an ass?"

Cade huffed, though humor warmed his features. "I'll do my best."

"Let me call Sheriff Archer and make sure the building is sound enough to walk through. If he says we can, we'll go after we're done eating."

Cade nodded his agreement.

An hour later, after talking to Kelly and the insurance company to let them know what he was planning, Cade followed him to Cassan. Cade knew where the bar was, but Dean was getting tired. He wanted to go home to bed and didn't argue Cade driving himself. He'd been up for nearly twenty hours already. On top of the stress of that morning and the full shift of the night before, he was fading fast.

Snow and mud had thickened to a raw sludge on the ground outside. It would become ice overnight.

"This was a good idea. There's no telling if this will be able to hold up under ice now, or more snow."

Cade stood at his shoulder, the small camera in his hand.

"Let's go around back. I don't know if this door is safe. The rear one is gone." It had been kicked in by the firefighters when they were battling the waves of the fire.

Cade followed as Dean led the way around the square structure, stepping under the yellow caution tape that was strung around the perimeter outside. A small side storage unit was charred but for the most part, intact. Cade started taking photos.

"Watch for weak spots and don't push on anything," Dean warned leading them through the door. "This goes right into the storage room. Trucks unloaded back here, so stuff is going to be spilled, and there's lots of exploded glass." He'd already seen most of what they were walking through before he'd finally left that morning.

Blackened wood was burned almost all the way through around where the door had once stood. The alcohol had added to the fire. It broke his heart seeing all the damage in the full light of day.

"What a mess," Cade muttered, carefully following in Dean's footsteps.

"Remember, don't move anything from where it is."

"Not sure I want to."

Water dripped from the ceiling, melted snow and water from who knew where, leaking through the now destroyed roof. Cade shot angles of the entirety as they went under it.

"The worst of it is the bar itself. I'm positive whoever it was used something like gasoline to get it going hot and fast." He pointed to the scorch marks on the bar, then to the streaks along the floor and the ceiling. "Once it got that high, the ceiling went up in flames. All dry, old wood. By the time the fire department got here, this was engulfed." He motioned above and around. Not a single bottle remained standing on display. They'd all been displaced or exploded.

"Man, Dean. You'd only locked up a little before this happened, right?"

"Maybe twenty minutes. The New Year's Eve party took forever to close down. They'd stopped drinking but getting them out of here..." He laughed with tired ruefulness. "Could've really used my bouncer last night."

Cade's hand with the camera lowered. He swept a hard look around the interior. "What if you'd still been here? Were you the last one out?"

"I sent Garret home about ten minutes before myself. I was counting the night's receipts for the deposit. Then I locked up and went home. I had literally just crawled into bed when the alarm company bothered to call me."

The building creaked ominously as cold wind bursts and water combined to make damaged wood shake and rattle.

Cade stared upward with him. "I see what you mean. That roof isn't going to hold up under any snowfall." Cracked and split beams proved the fire had been intense. Gaping spots exposed wiring and nails. It looked naked.

Dean took a step forward. "Look straight up." Cade did, bending to gaze where Dean pointed from the bar's damaged flat surface. "That hole is why I think there was something used to speed it along. There was nothing here on its own that would cause a pocket like that."

Cade straightened and took pictures of the bar beneath it and the hole itself. "These marks look even too, almost a perfect circle of the deep char."

"I thought the same thing." He groaned with realization. "And I bet I know what it was. A pile of rags. I had cleaning rags in the store room. I didn't think of them until mentioning them, but I bet they're gone." Dean sighed and rubbed his eyes.

"Tired?"

"Exhausted."

"Let me get some large view shots, and then we'll go."

"Sure," Dean replied, being careful to not touch anything. He was already coated in soot from walking around in it. A hot shower to warm up and get all this off his skin sounded pretty damn fantastic.

Cade took slow, methodical steps around the bar, even taking a panorama of the serving trench and all the damage it had sustained. All the decorative glass on the walls was destroyed. Hanging racks were knocked loose or simply shattered, leaving glassware dangling precariously. There wasn't an inch of space that hadn't been in flames, charred and burned to a crisp, sickening black. Dean's entire life, gone, in a matter of minutes.

Cade stopped in the middle of the floor. Tables were turned over with a few in pieces, chairs scattered around them, everything lying in puddles of water. He stepped over one, then stopped, twisting to focus on something.

"Did you hear that?"

Dean tipped his head. "What did you hear?" He didn't hear a thing. The wind. Dripping water, the little that there was. Nothing out of the ordinary.

"Footsteps." Cade spun slowly, as though following the sound. "And a car." He was scowling.

"Probably the cops outside wondering who's here. Let me—" was as much as he could say because there was a wet squelch of tires followed by the thunderous crack of a stud being wrenched out of place.

Chapter Six

Cade leaped across the interior, wrapping Dean into his body, taking them both to the damp ground with a crunching thud right as a huge chunk of the roof caved it. Dean gasped for breath, a low moan following. Cade covered as much as he could of the man beneath him, keeping him from being hit with falling shards and pieces of soggy insulation and debris.

Looking over a shoulder, heavy gray clouds now dominated the space where the ceiling and a portion of the wall had stood. Barely two feet behind where Cade had been taking pictures. The squeal of wet rubber hitting pavement registered, then it was gone in the distance.

"You okay?" Cade asked, listening, but hearing nothing else beyond the newer sounds of broken wood settling.

Dean coughed. "Yeah." He trembled beneath Cade, shook up regardless of if he was going to admit it.

Cautiously, Cade searched the room, then stood, offering a hand to Dean. "Better call your Sheriff friend."

Rough hacks were eventually followed by calmer breathing. "Are you okay? You were closer to the wall."

"I'm fine." Pissed, but fine.

When Dean pulled out his phone, Cade saw how much his hand trembled. "Let's get outside. No telling if anything will stay upright now." He'd feel a lot better if Dean wasn't standing in the middle of all that damage.

They walked around outside the opposite side of where the corner stud had been pulled. Cade spotted truck tire welts in the mud, along with the snapped stud and a length of shredded rope that had been left behind.

Dean spoke to the personnel on the other end of the phone, answering questions.

Cade slowly swiped a hand down his body, clearing bits that clung to his coat. Nearing Dean, he did the same. Brushing his back, soot smeared. "Damn."

Dean glanced at Cade when he raised a filthy hand.

"It'll wash." He turned off his phone screen. "Thank you." Confusion lay heavy between them.

"Any ideas on what is going on?"

Dean faced the broken stud. "Now? Not one." His chest rocked with a shuddering breath. "That was fucking intentional to the extreme. I have no idea."

A few minutes later, two county cruisers pulled in next to their cars.

"Dean."

"Sheriff Archer." Dean made introductions for Cade. "This is a friend of mine. We were inside taking the photo catalogue of damage I called about earlier when that happened." He motioned toward the pulled wood. "He heard somebody and we both heard the vehicle accelerate."

The Sheriff started writing. "Saucedo, go take a look at the tracks. See if we can get a good visual for make and model." The other officer went into his car and grabbed a camera of his own to take photos.

"How long have you been here?"

Dean glanced at Cade. "I really don't know. Less than an hour." Sheriff Archer was taking down notes.

"Do you think this has anything to do with the fire?" he asked Dean.

He looked over his shoulder at the quickly deteriorating building. "I'd have to think so. I don't know if the intent was to catch us inside or not, but I believe it was."

All three walked around the side to examine the view inward. The gaping hole displayed a huge portion of the interior now. "That's a support brace." The Sheriff scribbled some more notes. "If there had been enough weight above it, the whole roof would have come down. How close were you?"

Dean pointed. "I was there, about three feet in front of the bar. Cade was closer to the collapse, almost standing right where the fallout range is, there."

"Damn close," the Sheriff muttered.

Cade had to agree.

The Sheriff eyed Dean. "Who'd you piss off?"

"I have no idea." He sighed, discouraged.

Cade knew the man was exhausted. He shoulders slumped.

Officer Saucedo joined them with the rope bagged. "Is there anything for evidence inside?"

"No. The building was gone through this morning, after the fire department cleared it," Dean explained.

"Doubt we'll get much if anything but any little bit helps." Officer Saucedo gave Dean a sympathetic shrug.

"I'm going home. I need some sleep. If you hear of anything, let me know. I'll do the same."

They traded information then shook hands and the officers left.

Dean's phone jingled at him and he winced. "Shit. Hold on. I have to take this." He fished his phone out and answered. "Hi, Mom."

Cade smirked, hearing the absolute lack of desire in his voice to have to take that particular call.

"Happy New Year to you. No. I was at a friend's for breakfast." He scrubbed stiff fingers into shadowed eyeballs. "Gemini's burned down last night." He held the phone away from his ear as a loud, maternal squawking filled the air. "Are you done?" he griped. "I haven't been home *to* talk to you, so no, I haven't had time to call and tell you." He groaned. "Don't. I'm fine. You and Dad stay up there, okay? I'll call after I've gotten some sleep and tell you what I know. No, not much."

Cade zoned out as Dean gave a lackluster report. Even Cade knew he'd never get off the phone with that kind of a non-answer. He walked over to the tire tracks, crouching down to study them. Wide surface tires. Definitely for a pickup truck. Probably four-wheel drive. He examined the angle and the fall of the wood. Tracks of mud vanished into the distance on the asphalt, where the driver had simply kept going. He'd watched Officer Archer drive in that direction when he'd left, possibly hoping to follow the mud trail. Cade had his doubts it would be that easy.

Whoever had done this knew the piece they were pulling could bring down the roof. Someone who was familiar with the building, or at the least, had been inside. He watched a frustrated Dean verbally battle a now clearly harried parent. Getting a closer look at the tracks on the ground, he hunted for footprints. Finding those, he followed them from where he guessed the truck had sat waiting to the rear of the bar.

Cade's hackles rose. The person who'd tried to take down the bar had most definitely had one plan in mind. They'd snuck to the rear, deeper imprints showing where they'd stood in the mud and slush to either listen or to make sure there were people inside. The prints were clearer in the back. Boots. Smooth, like western cowboy boots. The slap of feet Cade had heard had been the driver being less cautious, knowing he had to hurry to catch his quarry—them— inside. He'd almost succeeded, on all counts.

Retracing his own steps, he waved over Dean.

"Mom. I have to go. I *will* call. I promise." He sighed, the sound of utter defeat. "Please. Let me find out before you spend the money to fly down here, okay? Okay. Thank you. Love you, too. Bye." He hung up the phone and shook his head. "All hell is about to break loose. I should warn Kelly my mother and father are flying in. They'll never get a moment's rest until this is figured out."

Cade put a hand on his shoulder. "Be thankful you still have yours, annoying as they are. They care enough to be here for you. That says a lot."

"Yeah, I know. I'm exhausted and my brain departed about twenty minutes ago." Relaxing by force, he put his phone away. "What did you want to show me?"

Cade walked with him from the start of the footprints. "Do you see this any differently?" he asked, after giving his own interpretation.

"Actually, no. But do you have any idea how many guys wearing shit kickers come here?"

"I know. The whole lot was pickup trucks the night I was here." He wasn't about to admit that was partially why he'd chosen to stop. He *knew* the crowd dynamics and hadn't been disappointed. Only now, Dean was paying for something, with everything.

Cade saw him rub at his eyes again. "Is there anything else we can do?"

Dean shook his head. "Not right this minute." Sorrow radiated off him in waves as he took in the destruction. "Daniel and I had worked so hard on Gemini's. It really hurts to see it gone now, too."

"What happened to your brother?" he asked gently.

"He was in the wrong place at the wrong time. Tried to break up a fight and was shot."

"Shit," Cade managed, almost choking on the deep gasp.

"It's why I'm still here and didn't go home to Michigan. Mom really wanted me to when that happened, and now? She's going to do everything short of blackmail. We pooled our resources after college to go into business for ourselves. I know. Why a bar?" He slid his hands into his coat pockets, taking his time to circle to the front of the building. "Believe it or not, neither of us really drink, or got drunk. Even in school. But it's one of the few recession proof businesses out there. There's always money for liquor. We had plans to buy this, and trade up when we had some financial stability. Then he died." Dean stared outward, though Cade could tell his thoughts were deep inside. "I couldn't bring myself to sell. This was ours. And it's all I really have — had — left."

Cade swept an arm around his waist and gave him a supportive hug. "I'm sorry."

"It still hurts, but I had something of his, of ours, in Gemini's."

Cade spotted the tear that slipped from Dean's lower lashes. Surprisingly, Dean didn't try to sweep it away, or hide it. A man not scared to show his feelings. That told him a lot about the man on the inside. And the depth of affection he still felt for his brother could be heard in every word.

"If he was your twin in every way, then I know he was an amazing person."

Dean rested his head on Cade's shoulder, leaning for support. Cade doubted he realized he was doing it.

"I don't know what I'm going to do. He's gone. Gemini's is gone."

Cade knew he was emotionally wrecked and exhausted on top of it. The day was catching up to him. "Let me drive you home. You shouldn't be behind the wheel this tired."

"Sure. I can get a neighbor to help me get my car in a few hours."

They made sure Dean's car was locked, then he poured Dean into his truck. "Just tell me where I'm going."

Dean navigated them into Cassan and down a side street. Cassan didn't look much larger than Silo. A town that was more community than bustling metropolis. Pavement turned into dirt road as he followed directions. Divided lots with grounded trailers appeared. Mostly single-wides with a few doubles tossed into the mix. Short fences or chain link separated yards. Yards filled with snowmen. It made him smile to see them all. He could imagine the kids and the havoc they would cause to make those stacks of snow.

Pulling into a driveway, he waited for Dean to make the next move. The house wasn't the cream of the crop on the street, but it wasn't in bad shape by any means. "Not what I pictured."

Dean snorted. "Why spend huge bucks on a house, when all I really need is a roof?"

"Did you share this?"

"No. I bought this after Daniel died." He fiddled with the buckle. "I appreciate your help today. I know I said thank you, but I mean it. You saved me again." He grinned loosely. "You're getting way too much practice at it for my liking."

Cade reached but his hand halted midair. "I owe you an apology, a big one, for earlier today."

"Forgotten." Dean hit the release on the belt.

"It's not that easy." He looked around at the fairly quiet street. "Can we talk inside?"

Dean shrugged. "Sure."

Cade followed, wondering how he was going to fix that morning's fuckups, and what he was going to say. *How much* he was going to say.

Dean unlocked the front door and let Cade in to shut it behind them. He unclasped his coat and hung it on a single standing rack, checking the smears on the back. "I'll have to take this to the cleaners. That is nasty." He faced Cade. "What did you want to say?"

Cade swallowed, actually feeling it when Dean's gaze locked with his. His toes tingled. *His fucking toes.* "I don't know how to do this," he finally pushed past his lips.

"What? Be friends?" Dean's brow furrowed.

Cade closed his eyes, reopening them a few seconds later. "No." He stiffened his spine, both physically and mentally. "Being gay has never been an option."

Dean's eyes narrowed. "It's not an option."

Cade avoided that stare; it knifed straight through him. *Fuckup number three hundred and twelve.* "No, it's not. But I tried to make it one." He shoved his hands into coat pockets to hide the fists he was making. "I refused to be gay, so I wasn't," he explained. At the least, he'd refused to allow any interest in men. Too much he still had to sort in his own mind. He only hoped he could make a sound argument to get Dean's forgiveness.

Dean canted his head to the side. "Refused? Is that even possible?"

Cade huffed. "I can see you have never visited the land of denial."

"No, I've known since Daniel and I were kids. Why would you do that to yourself?"

"Too many reasons," he admitted. "At least for right now."

Dean crossed his arms. "Not that tired. Try me."

Cade now wished he hadn't been so quick to start this. Wouldn't a solid apology have been enough? Now it was too late. Time to own up.

"My brother, for one. We've always been a tag team of sorts. One-upmanship was invented for us. He's found his mate...soul mate," he quickly corrected. Dean wasn't the only one feeling drained. Cade felt like he'd already gone rounds with Chris. Now… He had to be careful how to approach this. There was a shitload more to this, and so much at risk. "And I'm the last one standing. Again."

"Ah. When you say you're last, that's what you mean. You're the youngest."

"Yeah." He stretched his shoulders, trying to alleviate the building tightness. "So, there's that. And I want children. I need a woman, a wife, for that."

"No you don't."

Cade groaned. "Okay, okay. Alternatives, I get it. But that's the tip of the whole iceberg. The two largest reasons." At least two that he was willing to admit to.

"So you felt to be equal and then better than your brother, you had to find a woman? Do you really think Chris feels that way?"

"No," he replied in confusion.

"Then you have no reason to either." When Cade opened his mouth, Dean cut him off. "Look, if anyone understands that sibling rivalry tie, I do. But hiding who you are is wrong. You have amazing brothers and an incredible family. I can guarantee not one of them will look at you differently…okay, maybe shocked, but not *different* if you finally start being true to yourself."

"I don't know how to be gay. I don't even look gay!" He growled in exasperation.

A snicker and a raised eyebrow chastised him. "Oh? I look gay, do I? What gave it away? My rainbow farts?"

Cade blurted a laugh.

"No, I know. It was my trail of gold glitter, wasn't it? Did I have too much swish today?"

Cade cupped his chin to cover his mouth, chortling heartily. He turned away. "Stop!"

A firm tug on his elbow brought him front and center. "So what gave it away?" Dean asked with concerned gentleness. The absolute lack of anger was almost Cade's undoing.

Gasping, he took a few panted breaths. "Honestly, I thought you were straight until you said you weren't. Just very open-minded," he said when he could speak normally. "Still doesn't help me understand the *how* of it."

"I can't help you there."

That surprised Cade.

"It's too personal. It's a journey. Only you get to experience it." He scooted closer a couple of inches. "But unless this whole train wreck of you being an unmitigated asshole has been a product of something else, and not me, I can share that journey with you."

Cade's heart tripped. Green eyes impaled him. The fear that Dean didn't like him, wasn't attracted to him, was smashed to little bits beneath that stare. He couldn't define what he'd been more scared of: being proven a fool, or baring himself after decades of refusing to acknowledge what he felt.

"Close your eyes."

Cade blinked. Then shivered.

"Do it," Dean commanded quietly.

Cautiously, Cade did. Fingernails bit into his palms where they remained curled in shuddering fists in his coat pockets. Blood rushed through his veins. Anticipation, and a hint of wary fear roiled inside his chest like a pending storm.

"Relax," Dean offered. "Slow, easy breaths."

A small shiver slipped under Cade's skin at the timbre of his voice. He *wasn't* cold.

He realized with no small amount of shock that it was turning him on, hearing him, finding his scent between them. Hearing Dean's own slow breathing.

"Relax."

The touch, when it happened, was feather light. A stroke of skin over his lip. He didn't know if Dean was kissing him, or if it was a fingertip.

He realized he didn't really care which it was.

"Still okay?"

Cade gulped, a harsh, hollow click following. He nodded when his voice couldn't be found.

"Keep your eyes closed. No pressure." More of the light caress. "Has any guy ever touched you?"

"No," he whispered hoarsely.

"And you've never, either?"

He shook hard, rocking his stance.

"Easy. It's okay. Take your hands out of your pockets. Leave your eyes closed."

Stiffly, he managed to do as Dean asked. Harsh panting filled his ears. A needy void that had grown like a black hole over several months was suddenly calming. Dean continued to touch him, traced his lower lip, then his upper. Cade swore he was seducing him. The whole experience was surreal.

"Are you still hiding?" he asked kindly. "If this is what you've been missing, why fight it?"

"Because—"

"That argument is invalid. Try again." Wry humor. He couldn't see it, but he heard it.

"There's more that you don't know," he finally admitted. *So damn much more.*

"I know. This is a big step to make. It's a brave step. But lying about who you really are hurts yourself the most." The light tease of skin to flesh didn't stop, didn't speed up. "Do you trust me?"

Cade trembled. "Yes."

"Open your eyes."

Disoriented, he did. Dean still stood before him. Cade swore he felt body heat though he'd moved no closer. Gentle fingers ghosted over Cade's lips in butterfly sweeps, letting him see what he'd been doing. Then his hand fell away. Neither blinked for several heartbeats. Dean watching for something Cade didn't know, and Cade waiting for the unknown. When it happened, he almost short circuited.

Dean tilted to close the distance between them and pressed warm lips to Cade's.

He stiffened in shock. His immediate reaction was to shove him away, to deny, but he caught himself.

Barely.

A flicker of eyelashes proved Dean had caught the lightning swift battle. He made no noise, made no demands. It was simply pressure. Warmth. It felt...*different.* Firmer. There was the rougher brush of skin. Staring into Dean's eyes was like staring over the edge of a steep cliff.

And Dean didn't move. Not forward, not away. Sharing space and breath. The next action would be Cade's choice.

Heat replaced shock as time stood still. A heat unlike anything in his life exploded beneath his skin, bone deep. Slowly, his tripping heart found a rhythm.

And with the knowledge that Dean was as steady as a rock in this decision, he let his eyes close and he returned the kiss.

Chapter Seven

Dean watched and waited. He couldn't push, no matter how desperately he wanted to shove the man he kissed into the door behind him and pin him there as he learned the contours of his mouth like a cave of secrets.

Then, Cade gave in. The tension that held him stiff and trembling melted away. The shape of his lips grew heady, drugging. His eyes drifted shut and a slow sigh filled the silence.

It was Cade who surprised him by taking the initiative of the next step. While Dean was staying passive using only his mouth to hold contact, not wanting to shock him too deeply with the newfound discoveries, Cade lifted a hand and ran tentative fingers through the hair above his ear, like he was testing the feeling, testing the privilege. Dean leaned closer, encouraging his exploring. The firm stroke felt divine.

It was with deep reluctance that he pulled away from the kiss. He waited to see what Cade's reactions would be.

"I guess that answers that question," Cade said, his voice rumbling with a sexy undertone that helped to alleviate Dean's darker worries. The pure vibration also sent a rush of need through his frame. "Definitely like that."

Dean smiled in relief. "That's good to know. I liked being on this end of it."

Cade touched fingertips to Dean's jaw, a connecting touch. "Why don't you get some sleep? I'll download the photos I took and send them to you."

Dean supposed that was his way of putting a little space between them, giving himself a chance to regroup and digest. Cade frowned next, and then Dean found out why.

"I'm on shift this week at the veterinary clinic. Be careful, especially around Gemini's. Let me know what they say about the footprints behind the bar."

"I will. I'll call the arson investigator in the morning." Along with everyone who deserved one of Dean's boots up their collective asses. He noticed Cade was following the light, random flow of fingers to Dean's jaw, a sense of wonder in everything. "You in there?"

"I don't think so. Everything I knew for twenty-eight years has been completely rewritten."

"Does it feel wrong?" Dean asked. "Are you going back into hiding?"

Cade slowly raised from the stroke of those fingers to meet Dean's gaze. "No, and no. This is a step that can't be erased. It'll take time to adjust, that's all." A slow sigh escaped. "There is so much you need to know, I don't have any idea where to begin."

"Start here, now. One day at a time."

"I think I'm going to take that advice," he replied. "Can I try it again, make sure?"

"A kiss?" Dean chuckled throatily, warmth filling him when Cade gave him a hesitantly hungry expression that could only be read in one way.

With a firm hand on his shoulder, he backed Cade up to the door. "In case your legs start to feel weak," he warned.

"My legs?" He shook his head. "Not a fainting woman."

"I sure hope not," Dean replied with a bit more growl of his own in it. Cade's eyes flashed, then darkened. The speed with which Cade grew aroused stole his breath away. It sank deep into Dean's blood, knowing he made Cade feel like that. Being his first encounter was making him drunk to want more.

Dean threaded a hand under the heavy fall of his bound hair. He wanted it loose so badly, but knew today wasn't the day. "Find a comfortable place for your hands." Cautiously, they framed Dean's hips. He groaned quietly. "Perfect." He straddled Cade's thighs, locking them chest to chest, groin to groin. "How does that feel?"

"Unbelievable," Cade answered. "Unusual."

"It gets so much better."

"Yeah?" Cade replied on a slow breath.

"Oh, yeah." He wasn't going to point out that it felt like this with Cade still in his coat. The difference of skin to skin or merely less clothing might be too much to handle.

Dean found Cade's lips, coaxing him into a stronger kiss than their first. He couldn't wait for Cade's confidence to come to life and want to take control, but for now, Cade's kiss was the best known to all of history.

* * * *

Cade clipped Rufus' toenails, then gave him a roughing pat on the head. "He's all set for the next year." The German Shepherd panted, wagging his tail now that his feet were back on the floor.

"Thanks for doing those, Dr. Rose." Dawn coiled up the leash clipped to his collar.

"It's not a problem. At least we can do his. There's a poodle we have to muzzle. He absolutely hates his feet being messed with."

"Poor thing." She petted her animal, smiling now that he was happy, done with all his annual shots. "I know this is in bad taste to do here, but I told myself if I could, I would."

Cade put the clippers in the drawer. He turned around and found her handing over a slip of paper.

"Could you call me sometime?"

Cade sensed by the anxious nervousness in her eyes, she'd taken a huge step to make the effort to ask him. "I'm sorry, Dawn." He curled his hand over hers, folding the paper under her fingers. "I'm involved with someone." And that was his story until this whole situation with Dean blew up in his face. He didn't have blind faith in his wolf, but he couldn't deny that he liked the man. What he was doing, where this was going between them, remained a question mark.

"Oh." Her shoulders sank inward. "I'm sorry," she murmured.

"It's okay. No harm in asking, right?"

She looked up from dejected eyes. "It's hard."

"It is." He opened the exam room door for her. "Oddly, I'd say quit looking. Don't give up hope, but focus on something else. It seems for those I know when they do that, what they're looking for almost falls on them."

She laughed at him kindly, losing the dejected air. "Falls, huh?"

"Like from out of the blue," he shared, glad she was smiling for real. "Lyla will get you checked out."

This time she offered a hand only to shake. "Thanks again, Dr. Rose."

"You're welcome." He let her go around the corner then he snuck to the office to check his phone. He'd been checking it during the day for any messages from Dean. This time, *finally,* the message icon sat in the corner. His heart kicked into his ribs as anticipation made his fingers shake.

Call when you're done. Det took one look and said arson. Details at eleven.

That didn't surprise Cade in the least. He tapped out a quick question of his own. *Any ideas on the truck?*

There was a lengthy pause before he got more. *Not really. The tires were factory. Narrows it down to about 5000 trucks in the county.*

Cade could imagine the disappointment in that. *Okay. Will call in a few hours.*

There was no return answer. Cade sighed and slid the phone into coat pocket. "Damn."

At least the detective had been prompt considering the New Year holiday. Now if they could get to the bottom of the rest of it. It chilled him that someone had made an attempt to catch Dean in the roof collapse. Was it luck that they'd been found there, or was someone watching for Dean? Waiting for him? Was someone out for blood?

The bar had been arson. Someone had meant to hurt him with that. Cade crossed his arms where he leaned against the office desk. Now someone was taking it further. Cade wasn't going to say attempted murder. Not yet. The possibility of it made him edgy regardless. He couldn't swear it was the same person, either. For all he knew, the fire could have been a prank caused by one of the kids he tossed before Christmas, wounded ego issues. The collapse, though… That was something that went far further than disgruntled. That was attempted murder in his mind. He had kept that opinion to himself that morning. No sense in adding to Dean's stress.

He really hoped the police did a thorough job with the investigations. Cade didn't like the variables at play between Dean and Gemini's.

Cade was surprised when he drove up to his house that evening to find Dean parked at the curb, sitting on the car's trunk. His shoulders were tucked in tight, his hands buried into coat pockets. Cade wasn't sure, but it looked like he was singing. The fact that Dean would do that, unabashed and unconcerned to who may witness, made him smile.

He glanced to the ground at Dean's side and barked a short laugh. A plastic bag was buried into the snow. He was sure he could guess what was in the bag. Dean hopped off the car and hooked the bag loops with fingers when he turned into the driveway.

"Been here long?" he asked, getting out of the truck.

"Ten minutes or so. Not long enough to panic your neighbors."

Cade led the way indoors. They both hung up coats. "So, how'd today go?"

"Well, after I reamed out the alarm company, they've agreed full cooperation with the investigation." Dean sauntered into the kitchen and placed the beer in the refrigerator. Grabbing two, he handed one over to Cade.

"Come on. I have to change. Keep talking." He popped the top and drank. He preferred ales, but it was wet and tasty. Placing the beer on the dresser, he grasped his scrub top and tugged it over his head to toss in with the rest of his dirty laundry.

He thought Dean had followed, but he wasn't saying anything. Facing the doorway, he found out why. He was staring with utter shamelessness at Cade.

"I'm sorry. What was the question?" Dean took a full draw from the bottle.

Cade chuckled. "Alarm company," he prodded.

"Uh… Right. So apparently, they'd waited it out to see if an animal had tripped the alarm. Something in the roof, or even one of us returning, since the codes for the night had been entered not that long before everything went to shit. Then the fire codes went off, and that was when they passed *We fucked up* and went right to *Oh shit*."

"So it really was their delay in procedure?"

"Yeah. They wanted to see if they could reset the alarm electronically, and so the delay to contact the Sheriff was compounded."

"Man, that sucks so hard."

Dean sighed, shifting to lean with a shoulder to the doorframe. "Anyway, so the first part of it is squared away and being handled."

"And the truck?"

"That's where I have no ideas."

Cade toed off his shoes then shimmied out of his waist pants.

"Damn."

Cade looked up at the disappointed curse. "What?"

"You're wearing sweats under them."

Cade shook his head, laughing quietly at the man.

"Hey, don't hate me for hoping." Dean gave him a wicked grin. "Unless you're not done? Because I can definitely wait until you are."

Cade stood in his bedroom in a long sleeve Henley and black sweat pants. Sweat pants that were loose enough to not hide jack shit. "Well, I should put on something clean." *Damn. Did I just flirt with him?*

"Please. Don't let me stop you." Lashes lowered over heated eyes full of dare. An insolent dare that left no doubt to the challenge he was laying at Cade's feet. Need pulsed through his groin at the nonchalance reaching out to him.

Cade had changed clothes plenty of times with men around. He knew he and Quade both had physiques that many wished they could have. Chris was the same, a couple of inches shorter, but very solid. Broad in the shoulders and chest.

Only this time, with Dean looking at him, he *felt* the impact of that focus. Women had flocked to him. He'd never been short of attention from the softer sex. If men had looked at him, Cade had been oblivious. He hadn't looked for it in return. Denial, blatant refusal, whatever it amounted to.

He couldn't break away from the fire in Dean's eyes.

Cade's fingers twitched. "I... I turn you on that much?" He wasn't *nervous*, exactly, but it was so new. He didn't want to misread signals.

Dean swung the bottle in his fingers lightly by its neck. "Cade, if I thought you were ready, I'd blow you and fuck you until the sun went down — tomorrow."

Cade's heart jumped into his ribs. *Clearly not misreading shit.* No one in his life had spoken to him so bluntly in describing what they'd do sexually. Graphic detail in what they wanted. What surprised him more, when maybe it shouldn't, was now he was imagining what it would all feel like. "Is it different from a woman?"

Dean's shoulder rolled. "Wouldn't know. Never been with one."

Cade made himself move to the side of the room, to his closet, digging out a fresh pair of jeans. "Not even a kiss?"

"Kissed, yes. I made mistakes growing up, figuring out who I was."

"How could it be a mistake?" He held his change of clothes in a tight hand.

"Ever knowingly do something simply to not hurt someone else's feelings?"

Cade nodded.

"That's how I know. I kissed her just to spare her feelings. That was when I knew I'd rather be kissing a guy."

Cade could understand that. "So not a mistake."

"Maybe. Maybe not." He sipped at his beer, the bottle balanced lightly between strong fingers. "It's history."

Dean placed his nearly empty bottle next to Cade's and walked across the room to him. "Relax. I have patience, and control." He fisted the fabric of Cade's shirt and worked it upward.

Cade tossed his jeans to the bed to accommodate, raising his arms high.

"God, but you're built like a brick shithouse."

"You're not exactly a beanstalk, either, you know."

Dean arched an eyebrow. Pleasure glowed outward at the compliment. "Glad you approve."

Cade couldn't help himself, leaning into Dean's body heat, he hunted for and found the musk of warm skin. When his arms were free, they dropped to Dean's hips on their own.

Dean tossed the shirt. The flicked tease of lips skated over Cade's throat. Not only was it an unusual experience, an adventure in height, scent, and touch, but it wasn't normal for him to be the receiver. He led with women, was the aggressor, the alpha.

He whined low in his throat when Dean nipped lightly with teeth at his pounding pulse. His head canted to the side in what felt like a natural allowance. It didn't feel like a weakness to him at all. It felt…like heaven.

Dean moaned gently in approval, the heated sucks not slowing down one iota. Palms floated over Cade's chest and he shivered, skin tightening in waves. Thumbs circled his nipples, work-roughened pads causing a friction that burned nerves to sizzling sensitivity. Cade wrapped his hands around Dean's waist, bringing him closer, bumping dick to dick.

He gasped. Flesh pulsed. There was a tug on his hair, then he felt the wave as it fanned out over his naked back.

Dean moaned, stroking fingers through it as soon as it was loose.

Desire spun, coiling and snapping through his body, filling his veins. He cupped the back of Dean's head with a risen hand and brought him forward.

There wasn't an ounce of hesitation in his actions. There was absolutely zero doubt.

He took what he wanted.

The whimper of need that slipped from Dean was stronger than any aphrodisiac. It was deep, rumbled, and pure sex. Cade didn't fight what he wanted, what happened next. With fingers knuckle deep in Dean's hair, he tipped him closer, slicing between his lips with an advancing tongue.

Dean mimicked him, fisting Cade's loose strands like a rope. The kiss instantly became a passionate duel. Conqueror and conquered. Dean challenged him stroke to demanding stroke before finally giving Cade what he desired.

Submission.

A firm hand gripped at his waist, pinning Cade body to body with Dean. The strength behind it was assured, not tentative. Not soft in the least. Not the hold, not his kiss.

He broke their kiss reluctantly, trembling as his heart thudded with a bruising force.

The wolf was right. Dean was his mate. Never in his life had he felt this intoxicating need. Desire and tenderness, and want, but not a need that burned like lava raging through his body. He craved more, craved everything. It didn't faze him that he didn't know what that *everything* was. That was the least of his concerns. The physical side of a bonded mate would happen in its own time.

And that was the fact that coldly dashed the rush of lusting euphoria he'd been drowning in.

Both were panting when they separated. While his wolf may be smugly quiet, he had no idea how to break that truth to Dean. He could accept and learn to love him. The way Jamie had with Chris, and Maya with Quade.

Or it could make Cade the creature of nightmares.

He leaned to rest forehead to forehead, keeping contact. The hand that had been happily buried in hair slid to Dean's jaw, learning the rougher texture, the shape. Where would he be today if he hadn't denied himself all these years? He wanted children, but finding and claiming a mate were suddenly such larger issues.

Cade had never imagined what it would feel like to have the one he needed fear him. The thought of it now terrified him.

How did Dean get under his skin so fast?

Cade's thoughts were slammed to a screeching halt by Dean's mouth finding nerves to tease again.

His eyes drifted shut, drawn into the river of sensation.

"You're thinking too much," Dean murmured, breath and lips brushing flesh.

Not about what you think. Not about this. No. This felt incredible. This was swiftly becoming the least of his worries. Cade agreed though, thinking at a time like this was overrated. Palms ghosted over his body to dig under the waist of his sweats. Dean grasped a side in each hand and brought them closer still.

Cade grunted softly. It was unusual for him to be with someone physically strong enough to maneuver him effortlessly. Not that he was hating what Dean was doing. If anyone had ever paid him a fraction of this level of oral attention, he couldn't remember. Dean hadn't stopped nibbling, licking, or kissing since he'd started.

He roamed from a shoulder upward to tease at an earlobe, then slid downward, only he didn't stop at the shoulder where he'd been lavishing. No, Dean and that taunting tongue kept going south. Cade hissed when he swirled over an unbelievably sensitive nip.

This was so unlike anything else he'd experienced. The abrasion of new growth stubble razed skin as they moved and bumped together. He'd always thought he'd lacked sensitivity across his chest. There'd been so little that aroused him when it came to his chest and nipples.

Unless he'd become possessed, that was not the problem now. It was like every woman's touch, every kiss, every caress had been felt through cotton. *So all this time it wasn't me, it was who I was with.* Talk about a glaring epiphany. He'd never suspected. How could he when he'd never been in this situation? When he'd convinced himself that there was only one way, and it didn't involve another man? This was only one more bit of proof that Dean was the one. Only his mate would affect him so deeply.

A shudder rolled down his frame when lips and tongue became teeth. He gripped at Dean's hair. Tugging the man upward, he latched onto his mouth, thrusting in ownership, to taste. There was the tang of the beer on his tongue and an underlying earthy flavor that was all Dean. Every breath rocked them together, molded them. The heat seared Cade.

He wasn't sure who moved, but three steps had them against the edge of the bed, then his knees buckled. Dean went down with him, beneath him, and neither seemed in a rush to change that.

Cade crawled over Dean. The faint thud of shoes hitting floor preempted the unified shift of making an attempt at getting them on the bed. They stopped when it was close enough for Cade.

A low groan rose up when he centered himself over Dean's length. Cade angled above him on a braced palm and tugged on Dean's shirt. He had to see skin. Had to know what it felt like.

Dean managed to help unbutton the top few of the flannel, then worked it over his shoulders and head. He flicked it away, gazing up at Cade with inviting eyes.

"Disappointed?"

Cade stilled above him. "Why would I be?"

"Not what you know."

Was he disappointed? He lightly ran a spread, seeking palm down Dean's chest, traveling from his collar bone to the meeting of his sternum, slowly mapping the differences, the texture, the solidness. Was he going to miss tits? The softness of a woman's body? The feminine scent?

He lowered to a supportive elbow on the bed, propped right over Dean's frame. He straddled a well-muscled thigh, intent on what lay in front of him. Sensations fed upward from his learning touch. The firmness of muscle beneath taut skin, the crisp-soft mat of hair that dusted Dean's chest and narrowed to a thin line to his belly button and beyond, the pounding of Dean's heart beneath flesh and bone barriers.

He threaded fingers into the dark wisps. Electric currents pulsed against nerves, and he did it again, testing.

A shuddering breath rocked his chest as desire raged, want and need fed by the simple touch.

"No," he whispered. "I don't think I'm ever going to be disappointed."

Dean raised a hand upward, cradling Cade's jaw. Grasping tenderly, he urged Cade lower.

Chapter Eight

Dean had lusted for this man on sight. Cade definitely came with his own brand of issues. He had known a few closet cases, men who refused to accept and hid in the shadows for whatever reasons, but this was the first time he'd found someone who'd denied their inner needs and desires to the point that no one suspected he was in fact hiding.

Dean released him from the kiss. "Could it be possible you're bisexual?" He didn't know why it didn't occur to him sooner.

Cade stilled above him. "I hadn't thought about it like that." Warm fingers brushed over Dean's chest to thread into his hair. "I wasn't forcing myself to be with women, if that's what you mean. I enjoyed them."

That's exactly what he meant. And he wasn't sure why it irked him.

"Does it matter?"

Dean realized he'd gone quiet, lost in his own head. "I don't know."

"It wouldn't matter to me if you had."

Dean tilted his head, pushing into the pillow to study Cade's thoughtful face.

"It's in the past. We can't change yesterday."

"True," Dean replied belatedly.

Cade slid to rest at Dean's shoulder, leaving one leg draped over the thigh where he'd been lying. Holding him in place. Dean had no interest in moving.

"It really doesn't matter." Cade snorted softly. "Trust me. By the time you know everything, it's *really* not going to matter."

"What everything? I know your family, what you do." *What's left?*

When Cade remained pensively silent, Dean tried to inch away. "Are you positive?"

Confusion furrowed Cade's forehead. "Positive?" He blinked, then, "Oh! No. I can't get sick." His lips pinched as soon as he'd spoken.

"Can't get sick? Ever?"

He hesitated, then shook his head jerkily.

"Cade…"

"Look, I *will* tell you. I promise, but not right this second. I'm not sick, nothing I can do to make you sick, or get HIV, or anything like it." Dean didn't stop him when he rolled to sit on the edge of the bed, his head cradled in his hands. "It's a big deal in my family."

"If you're loaded, I'm not the kind to take advantage of that."

Cade huffed derisively. "Wish we were, but no, not loaded."

Dean flipped sideways, resting his head against Cade's thigh at the edge of the bed to look upward into his face. "So why don't you tell me now?"

A shudder shook the man. "I want to," he whispered. "It would mean everything to me if you could accept what I am." A few minutes later, Cade straightened on the edge of the bed. His hands fisted to hang between his thighs.

"What you are? Like mixed race?" Dean was trying to figure it out, but he couldn't. He swore Cade and his brothers were as close to corn-fed Midwestern as anyone could get.

Cade scrubbed his eyes. "No, not in the way you're thinking, anyway." He twisted to meet Dean's stares. "I swear, I will tell you."

Dean didn't understand the underlying fear coming off Cade. Shaking fingers sifted into Dean's hair and brushed through it. This man had faced eight drunk frat boys single-handedly. What could possibly be so bad now?

Dean found Cade's hand with one of his own and tugged. "Get back here." He returned to where he'd been on the bed, waiting patiently, watching. After a small hesitation, Cade followed, stretching out beside him on the bed. Dean plied fingers through the long strands of hair at Cade's back. "If it's that important, I'll wait. Seriously got me curious, though." He supposed patience *was* going to be a virtue with Cade.

Cade slowly relaxed, melting into the bedding as Dean soothed him. An arm stretched across Dean's waist, holding them together. "Warm enough?" he asked.

"Mm hm." Pale eyes were closed. His firm chest rose and fell at a rhythmic rate. The strain of the last few minutes was gone. There was almost a languid easiness between them now.

Watching Cade rest was a study in beauty. He wasn't *beautiful* in the sense of classic reverence, but there was something very natural, very earthy about the man lying next to him that Dean was drawn to. Strong, rugged features were actually softened by his longer than average hair. Visually exploring the man, he took his time. There was a full moon tattoo on the backside of his upper left shoulder, a wicked portent of darkness and light in color and dimension, half hidden by a bank of rolling clouds. On any other, it would have been cliché, but the blended colors and shadowy depth in the design proved it was a well-thought out piece. It was what he had seen now that Cade had removed his shirt. He couldn't help but wonder if there were still more lurking under clothing. Dean wanted to trace the moon and follow the shimmery mounds of inky clouds with his tongue.

That wasn't all he wanted to do with his tongue.

"What's that sound?"

Dean raised his head upward to listen. Then groaned, plopping to the pillow. "My cell. Mom. Since the fire, she's been calling daily."

"Do they know you're gay?"

"Yes." He brushed light fingers into the wisps of dark gold over an ear. "They've known since before I had the balls to tell them."

"Was Daniel?"

"Yeah." He sighed a sorrowful breath. "They weren't disappointed. Well, probably a little. Mom wants grandkids."

"What about you?"

"I'm too young for grandkids," he replied evenly, though he poked his tongue into his cheek to not laugh.

Cade snickered. His eyes remained closed.

Dean traced Cade's ear, watching the flutter of muscles in reaction. "I've been neutral, I guess. I'm not going to marry someone to have them, and I'm not going to go it alone."

"So…if children happen after you're comfortable, you'd be okay with that?"

Dean thought about it. "Yeah, I guess that's a good way to put it."

Cade's eyes drifted open. "I want kids. Maybe not a baseball team, but at least two." Worry darkened the gray of his eyes. "I know it's a lot to ask up front, a lot to expect."

Dean smiled softly. "I'd rather know up front than get hit with those kinds of life changing decisions six or even twelve months down the road, especially if this becomes something between us."

"Do you want it to?"

"Do you think I'd be lazing in bed with a half-naked hunk *without* trying to jump your bones if I had other intentions?"

Cade didn't blink, his gaze growing heated in slow increments. "What kinds of intentions?"

Dean arched an eyebrow and scooted closer on the bed. Cade naturally covered him from their touching thighs to bare chests. Strong arms looped around Dean's pillowed head and cradled his shoulders until Cade was looking down at him.

"I get the feeling you're going to be a toppy bastard."

Cade grinned with a hint of evil. As though he *liked* that idea. "Is that a problem?"

"So long as you understand I expect a fair shake in doing the driving." Honestly, he *wanted* to have Cade melted under him. The lustful dream had turned into a real possibility.

Cade hummed, divulging little of his thinking.

Dean knew this was all new to Cade, but at least it didn't sound like he was completely against the possibility. It was all still an unknown for the other man. He hoped this didn't turn into a point of contention. Only time would tell what Cade could handle.

He roamed hands up Cade's sides, caressing smooth skin over ribs to grip fingers around strong shoulders. The pounding of his heart sped up as heat flared to life between them. Dean tipped his head, giving access to what the other man wanted.

He sighed, which morphed into a groan as Cade repaid the teasing kisses and bites he'd already given. Slipping a hand upward, he palmed the top of Cade's head, encouraging him for more, to take all he wanted.

Shocks and shivers ghosted over his frame. He pushed his legs against Cade's, holding tighter when he wound them groin to groin. Slow thrusts ground them together, languid, learning. He hoped it felt as good for Cade as it did for him.

Gliding a hand down Cade's side, the elastic of his sweats was no deterrent. Cade grunted, making Dean smile. He wiggled downward a little to get a firm grip. *Nice.* Cade nipped with sharp teeth in answer. A shock the size of Canada rolled down his spine, firing goose bumps in all directions.

Cade rubbed against his cheek. There was a rasp of skin, the scrape of teeth, then the teasing of a slow tongue.

Dean panted. "Driving me crazy," he managed between gasps.

Cade rose above him, to grudgingly roll away. Dean followed, stopping on a shoulder to study him at the sudden coolness. The other man was breathing heavily, his lips swollen from the profusion of kisses. Hesitant, Dean hovered a hand over one of Cade's resting on his chest, to cover it and squeeze. His heart relaxed when Cade squeezed in answer. "Everything all right?"

Cade swallowed. "Yeah." After a few minutes, he said, "Are you hungry?"

Dean held fingers in his grasp. Cade wasn't kicking him out. He'd take that as a good sign. "Wouldn't turn down food."

Cade's lips twitched. "You might. I'm cooking."

"Why don't you finish changing? I'll go see what has Mom's tail feathers up again." *Give him space.* It wasn't the first thing on the list of what he wanted to give, but Dean could wait. He *did* have patience. It looked like he was going to be using it plenty around Cade.

Cade rolled his head to gaze at him. Dean tried to read his expression. The only thing he knew for sure was he wasn't angry, or running. Cade arched and found Dean's lips for a small kiss. "I'll be right there."

Dean nodded and scooted off the edge of the bed, locating his shirt as he crossed the room. Swiping his beer off the dresser, he sauntered to the living room to find out what his mother needed.

* * * *

Cade changed into the waiting jeans and a fresh sweatshirt. When he went to bind his hair, he remembered feeling Dean's fingers running through it. On impulse, he left it swaying loose down his back. Taking a few minutes to dress helped calm the crying need of his body. He wasn't ready for that. He wasn't sure how much he would ever be ready for, either.

A lot had changed for him in the two weeks since he'd met Dean. The first hurdle had been cleared — admitting he wanted the other man. He didn't know if it had been a full-on case of denial or not, but the wolf had made its point. He had no idea if this situation even made him gay. All he knew was he *was* attracted. And wasn't that half the battle?

He found the other man still on the phone, so he continued to the kitchen. The house wasn't overly large, a fair two bedroom for the day when it was built. For a single man, the size of the home wasn't an issue.

Placing his beer to the side, he rummaged around in the fridge for something to make. Heating the oven, he prepped two slabs of ribs, letting them rest on baking sheets. He didn't have a lot of vegetables. They really weren't what he craved, but he had enough to throw together a green bean dish.

"Need any help?" Dean asked from the entranceway.

"No." He held up choices. "Cornbread or biscuits?"

"Cornbread."

"Good choice." Cade tossed the biscuits back into the fridge. "What did your mom want?" He started mixing the ingredients in a bowl for the cornbread.

"A bar update." He crossed his arms and rested on a shoulder. "I hope they start giving me answers soon. I can only hold her off for so long."

"What can she do?"

"Nothing, which I've told her a thousand times already." He grumbled quietly. "I know it's really her needing to be here."

Cade glanced in Dean's direction. "You didn't tell her about the roof, did you?"

"Are you kidding?" He groaned roughly. "She'd be here so fast, she'd leave a wake behind her. No way."

Cade poured the mixture into a dish, ready to bake. "There has to be some reason somebody would do that. It was deliberate."

Dean nodded. "I agree." His gaze went unfocused, his thoughts clearly his own. "But what part of it hasn't been deliberate?"

"I know," Cade replied, disheartened. "Have you had any problems?"

He glanced upward. "Like what?"

"I don't know. People following you?" Dean shook his head. "Have you been back by Gemini's?" Another negative. "And no problems at your house?"

"Other than being bored out of my mind, no."

Cade grinned. "I imagine you would be." He placed things in the oven to cook. "That'll take a little while."

Dean's phone buzzed again. He rolled his eyes. "At least it's not Mom." He turned to retrieve the phone.

Cade heard him answer then Dean reappeared.

"So you think they may be connected? To which? The fire or the collapse? I see." His brow furrowed. "When will you talk to them? Okay. Let me know. It's being handled by the insurance company, but if there's any way to tie anyone to the roof collapse… No, I understand. No…" Dean sighed with mild exasperation. "Why would I do something like that? I'm not going to chase someone down. That's not my job." Cade could tell his patience was growing short with the other person on the line. "Glad to know we can agree on that. I want the investigation closed so

I can move forward to rebuild. I can't do jack waiting for the insurance to sign off on it. In the meantime, I'm not making any income."

Figuring Dean would be ready for it after that particular phone call, he withdrew a fresh beer and popped the top on it.

"Okay, thanks. Yes, Detective Gentry is working up the final report to send out to everyone. Early next week at the latest was the last I'd heard. Fine." He tapped the phone and groaned. "Jesus H. Christ."

"Who was that?"

"The crime scene investigator. The roof collapse created another can of worms and Kelly turned it. Someone went out not too long after we left to take more photos, and confirmed the foot prints and tire welts. I guess they saw the same things we did."

Cade handed over the bottle. Dean accepted with a grunt of thanks, drawing a couple deep slugs before licking his lips and sighing in aggravation. "They think they have a lead on both and warned me not to go hunting for them." He shook his head. "Like I would."

"Who?"

"They didn't say. All he said was they have a couple of suspects to talk to. I've given so many reports in the last week, I swear I could write a book. Where I've been, who I've talked to. A ton of names, people I could vouch for being at Gemini's New Year's Eve. They've gone back through those names and gathered more. They've probably found every body that was there that night, drunk or sober. Between them, the insurance, and the alarm company, I'm about to punch something." He closed his eyes and growled. "I can't tell you how many times and ways they phrased the question to try to get me to admit to doing it. It might not have been much to look at, but it was ours, mine. Whatever." He drained the bottle and slumped to his spine against the kitchen doorway frame. He gazed at Cade with tired eyes. "I just want it over."

Cade reached for the bottle and tossed it, then walked over to Dean to stand in front of him. "It will be." He straddled the other man's legs, tugging him by the shoulders to wrap him close. "Why did they think you'd try to find this person on your own?"

"Apparently, there's some connection to the guy who shot Daniel. I don't know what. He wouldn't say." He bent, curling to rest against Cade's shoulder.

Someone from Dean's past. Someone who knew about Daniel. Someone who knew how to find Dean. Revenge? Mistaken identity? Cade repressed the shudder of apprehension. "And they think this person is what? Coming for you?"

"I don't know. The roof might have been coincidence and opportunity. Or the person who'd started the fire may have been watching, waiting for someone to return, and when it was me..." He sighed, slumping more. Cade knew this was wearing on the man. Simply not knowing was stressful. He remembered very well the hassle and stress Chris had been under when the vet clinic storage shed had burned down, and that had only been a loss of property, not an entire world gone up in flames.

"Did the detective think you were in danger?"

"No. Just said not to hang around the bar until this is solved."

"So someone is watching for you?" That's what it sounded like to Cade. Why else would he be warned to stay away from his own property?

"I don't know."

Cade kneaded the nape of Dean's neck, feeling the tension in his body and shoulders. Gradually, it released under his fingertips' ministrations. "Do you want to stay here tonight?" he offered. At least Cade could keep him close for a few hours. He really didn't like the insinuation that someone from Daniel's past was shadowing Dean, possibly even hunting for him.

His wolf growled quietly in answer to the thoughts. Someone was out to harm its mate. It pushed at Cade's soul, demanding he do something, anything, to keep Dean safe.

"I think I'd like that," he murmured sounding, at the least, a little more relaxed than ten minutes ago.

"What are you doing during the day while this is going on?"

"Not much. Watching TV, staying by the phone."

He didn't doubt that was boring as hell. Cade wasn't really good with waiting, either.

"Well, let's get through this week and see what Detective Gentry's final report has to say. If nothing else, with being removed from suspicion the insurance should release the policy funds and you can focus on that."

"That's what I'm hoping for. Just something to not have to think about the roof and what happened." Solid arms wrapped around Cade's waist. "You were the one they almost took out."

Cade nuzzled Dean's temple. He didn't gloat, but it was nice to hear Dean's worry for him. "It'll work out." Eventually.

Chapter Nine

After spending the night in the same bed, the rest of the week felt more hollow and empty to Cade than ever before. Dean had gone home to wait for any word about the investigation or the arson report, and Cade had continued his week at the animal clinic. It was one of the most drawn out weeks Cade could remember.

Disappointingly, Dean didn't come back to Silo for another sleepover, either. The nights were cold and seemed endless, even when he managed sleep. His wolf was already forming bonds to Dean, whether Cade was ready or not.

He tried to be congenial to patients.

Brothers didn't fare as well. Even Jamie was giving him a wide berth, which wasn't all that easy considering the size of the veterinary clinic. It made him feel that much worse that he was making life miserable for his brother-in-law because he couldn't be with Dean.

And if it was like this now, what was life going to be like later? If they completed the bonding? If he introduced him to the pack?

No, not if, when. He knew that was inevitable.

Unless he lost Dean.

The howl he heard rocked his ears.

Damn. The day could not end soon enough.

He barely took the time to change when his shift was finally over, layering clothes to be out in the cold. He needed his bike, and there was only one direction he was going to take.

The roads were still clear, thankfully. Tucking his hair under his helmet and jacket, he roared out of Silo on his ride. He'd even remembered gloves this time. He needed the rush, the wind, and focus. Needed to get this...*lust* under control. There was a *need* he didn't understand. A need to be with Dean. A need to be close to him. A hunger he hadn't ever tasted. It went deep, like he'd been infiltrated at his innermost marrow.

It had been steadily growing since the weekend. Since those kisses. The weight of the man held in his arms as they'd slept was a lingering memory. A sensation he'd hunted for every night that week. He snorted. *That* certainly hadn't helped his sleeping any.

Restless, needy, hungry. Was it any wonder Jamie had been giving him room? He understood what Cade was going through, probably better than Cade himself did. He grunted, his jaw tight with frustration. The crisp wind stole away each breath.

Maybe he should talk to Chris or Quade. Cade knew Chris had gone to get advice once from their alpha, Roman. He didn't know why he'd assumed finding his mate would be easy. It really should have been.

He'd never anticipated the curveball life had thrown at his head. In that, Chris had the advantage. He'd known what he'd liked since he was a kid. Cade... He sighed, the cloud of steam gone in a flash. Had he been hiding or was this simply something he was going to have to learn to live with and appreciate that he'd found his mate at all?

He spotted the burned out hulk of Gemini's not too far in the distance. On impulse, he slowed and rolled to the rear of the building, out of sight from passing vehicles or curious eyes. Unlatching his helmet, he rested it on the seat, taking a slow look around. The tape was still up, but sagging because of ice buildup. The hole in the outer wall was still there, as was all the debris the collapse had caused. A pattern of dull footprints wandered in and out of the entrance. Likely the investigators'. The smell of burnt wood had faded some.

Tilting his head, he listened, but only heard the quiet sounds of nature amid the creaks and shudders of the damaged building.

Being on the lookout for ice on the ground, he did a slow search around the rear, and then back up the side where the truck had sat before it had ripped out the support beam. More footprints cut swaths through the muck that had firmed under the cold. If there was any way to distinguish them by age, or person, it was lost on him. He hoped the investigators had found what they'd needed.

Returning to the motorcycle, he leaned on it and crossed his arms, looking at the building. What was he not seeing? What would bring this kind of anger to a man? Why would someone want to harm, and possibly kill, Dean? Once more the night before Christmas popped up in his memory. But who of those could be tied to Daniel's death? The more he thought about it, the less likely it seemed that anyone with a grudge and history would visit a place with a bad memory, especially for what they were doing that night.

Letting his gaze roam and wander, he saw the building, the parking lot, the dumpster, rough ground, and mounds of filthy snow and ice. He guessed that anyone digging for clues had searched the area.

But what a human might miss, a lupine nose certainly wouldn't. He dug his phone out of his pocket to silence it. No sense in letting it be obvious someone was hanging out around back. He stripped his jacket and laid it on the seat next to his helmet, doing the same with his sweater and undershirt. Bared to the waist, he walked behind the utility storage building and finished undressing, stuffing his socks in his boots to fold his jeans once they were off. He rested them neatly on the boots to keep them off the ground.

Crisp grass crackled under bare feet. The bite of the sharp chill was a shock to nerves. Listening to the silent world surrounding him, he let the wolf free, merging as their blood, their bones, their souls became one.

A hard huff of crystallized breath was followed by a fierce shake as the animal adjusted to the chill. He didn't let the wolf out often outside of pack runs, and Cade felt its wary confusion.

The animal scented the air. Char and mud, people and ash. Keeping a strong connection to the animal, he let it cautiously emerge from behind the shed. Alert and patient.

Time to do a little snooping.

* * * *

Dean put the car in park and shut the engine off. Staring at the burned out shell of Gemini's made something inside his chest ache. The sign that had hung near the door was dangling off a support, the electric cables limply draped to disappear somewhere on the ground. There hadn't been any windows. An old, rustic, wood building that had been through quite a few owners before he and Daniel had taken it over. He knew he had no reason to be there, but sitting at home waiting for people to dot their Is and cross their Ts was killing him. The longer he had to wait, the more it felt like the last memories he had of his brother were slipping through his fingers.

"I don't know what happened, Daniel," he whispered into the silence. The hole in the side felt like a punch to his gut. More caution tape had been hung, for all the good it did.

There was so much left unsaid, unanswered in what had happened here. Wrapped in his jacket, he wasn't ready to get out of the car. That gaping hole in the wall intimidated him. Someone had taken time, had made the conscious decision to cause that.

He snorted.

Like the fire hadn't been?

Only... He'd been feet from where the ceiling had fallen, Cade even closer.

Sheriff Archer had asked who he'd pissed off.

Dean wished he knew.

Sighing, he opened the car door and let it quietly click shut. The air was still, cold, any sunlight already fading. Wispy clouds were thinning, allowing the high moon to glow down on the world. It felt wrong to create a sharp interruption. There was almost a sense of calm to the air. Like nature was waiting to draw its next breath.

With his hands fisted inside his pockets to keep warm, he strolled along a wide path around the building, watching the ground, letting his vision skip every now and then to his surroundings.

His feet froze to the ground when he turned the corner.

A motorcycle sat in the graying dimness. The helmet and a few articles of clothing waited on it.

Dean frowned. He could swear that was Cade's bike. Walking closer, he spotted the black leather jacket. He didn't doubt it now.

Glancing around in confusion, he looked for the other man. A man who was obviously half-naked if all the clothes were his.

"Cade?" A chilled shiver strolled down his spine. What was Cade doing there? Where was he?

A scraped sound whipped him around to the darkened opening of the rear entrance.

Dean hopped back a step, startled to find himself not alone. And it wasn't Cade.

Gazing up at him were a pair of gray eyes surrounded by dark fur. Eyes and a muzzle then very slowly, a body materialized.

The dog whined.

"Hey, buddy," he tried calmly. He had no idea if the big thing was wild or not. It wasn't acting aggressive, just cautious.

It took a small step forward. Dean held his ground.

"Staying out of the cold? Not sure this is a good choice," he said. He wasn't sure how long they stood staring at each other before the dog inched through the doorway and darted out into the fields behind the property. Dean lost it pretty quickly in the thickening darkness.

"Cade?" Still no answer.

Dean frowned. Why was he here? His bike was hidden behind the building, and if he hadn't come to this side of it, Dean would have never known he'd been there. So why was he there and not wanting that to be known?

Dean leaned on a mostly unmarred spot of the storage shed.

Cade had better have a few answers ready when he decided to show his face.

* * * *

Cade waited and listened.

Dean didn't try to follow. He didn't hear the car start up again either, and after a few minutes, he realized why. The other man was waiting for Cade.

Shit!

He paced in slow circles in the tall weeds and frozen, dried grasses. This was *not* how he wanted Dean to find out about the wolf. He was grateful the man had thought he'd really only been a homeless dog, but fuck and hell.

How was he going to get to his clothes? How was he going to explain this to Dean? He'd hidden when he'd heard the car pull up. With the angle Dean had parked at, he could see right inside through the demolished hole in the side wall, so Cade had hunkered down and hoped he'd drive away again.

No such luck.

As soon as Dean had discovered his motorcycle and knew he was there, Cade knew he'd start looking for him.

Silently, he was cussing in ways that would have had his mother after him with a bar of soap.

After another ten minutes in the freezing cold, he couldn't make Dean suffer. It was getting colder now that any sunlight was gone.

"Cade! Come on. It's fucking cold as shit out here. Where are you?"

He sighed in defeated acceptance, hanging his head.

With his tail and his head low, he emerged out of the field and dragged his ass toward the shed. He could stay hidden, but he'd still have to explain what he'd been doing there. He'd tried to make the best decisions during his lifetime. He could only hope this was one of them.

"Hey," Dean called gently, the one word full of genuine concern.

Lifting his line of sight, he landed right on a pair of green eyes that were pinned on him as he approached.

"It's cold out here, huh? I bet you're freaking cold, too." He squatted down and let a hand hang limp off a knee, knuckles lightly bent in offering.

Cade let the wolf greet him. Let him run his face all over that hand. He even licked at Dean's cold fingers once.

He couldn't hide the terror that this was all he'd get of the man once he knew the truth.

"I don't know what you are, a hybrid maybe. At least you're friendly." He continued to talk in a soothing, calm voice.

Cade would have chuckled if he'd been on two feet. *No, not a hybrid.* At least not the kind Dean was thinking of. After a long nuzzle against his outstretched hand, he backed up and stared right into him.

He hardly moved, didn't twitch, didn't blink. He hoped Dean made the connection when he saw him face to face again.

Almost sick to his stomach with what he was about to do, he backed up and slipped behind the shed to dress. On two feet.

A few minutes later he heard, "Cade! Come on man. There's a poor dog out here freezing to death. I'm about to take him home with me and leave your sorry ass out here. What the hell are you doing here anyway? Where are you?"

Cade shook his head. *Wish you would take him home.* He stomped into the second boot and stood straight.

He drew a slow breath. Cold bit at bare flesh again. It must've dropped ten degrees in the last half hour.

"I'm here," he said, walking out from behind the shed. At least there was enough moonlight to not scare the poor man out of his skin.

Dean jerked away from the shed. "Shit! Where'd you come from? Why didn't you answer?"

Cade's jaw clenched tight. He reached for his shirt and tugged it over his head. "I want you to just listen for a minute," he replied.

"To what?" Dean's anger was on the rise. "What the hell are you doing here? Why were you hiding? Why didn't you answer me? Why are you walking around naked?"

He pulled on the sweater. He ignored every single one of his questions. "What color were the wolf's eyes?"

"What? The dog? You saw it?"

"Dean." He scrubbed a hand down his face. "Christ. Where do I even start?" he muttered.

"Just tell me what you're doing here first." Dean stood stiffly, only a foot or two away.

"I came to see if there were any clues that could have been overlooked." Unfortunately, he hadn't found a single thing. Not a hair, not a left behind mistake. Nothing. And his want to help may have ruined his entire future. He tied back his hair. "I'm asking: What color were the wolf's eyes?"

"That was a dog, if you saw it. Wolves don't live around here."

"Dean," he said with a hint of sorrow and exasperation. "Please." He hadn't looked at the other man yet. His stomach was a corkscrew tight mass of knots.

"I think they were gray. Wait. Aren't most dogs' eyes like brown or maybe blue? It did look a little like a malamute or maybe a shepherd mix." He snapped his jaw shut. He glared at Cade. "Quit that! Tell me what you're doing here, at night, hidden, and for the game point, half-naked!"

"I told you, I was searching. As for the half-naked…" He let out a slow, controlled breath. It was a whitish stream in the frozen world before it dissipated. With a wealth of caution and just as much apprehension, he faced Dean. "Look at me, Dean. Look closely."

Dean sneered.

Cade didn't move, and he didn't blink.

Gray eyes locked on green.

"Picture the wolf. He's a near black with gray eyes, right?"

Uncooperative, Dean nodded. "If you saw it—"

112

"Dean," he growled. He wanted to get the man out of the cold, but didn't dare force him to make the connection, not on this. It scared the shit out of him to have to push like this as it was. This *really* wasn't how or when he wanted to share the truth with the man. The bonds were still forming, weak. One mistake and it would be all over for him. He moved a few inches closer. "Just…try. Please?" he begged. "Look at me and try."

Dean's expression didn't change. "You are just as insane as I'd first thought. I don't know where your mind is, man, but it's fucking freezing. There is a lost dog out here somewhere, and you're where you're not supposed to be. Here."

"Let me come home with you and I'll bring the dog with me," he offered.

"On your bike?" Dean tossed his hands in clear disgusted disbelief. "If you're not going to tell me the truth, fuck off. I don't need headaches like this."

"Dean." He closed his eyes briefly and tried to calm his heart. "I *can* explain. I… I'll show you." He was losing ground so fast here. He really wanted to get the other man out of the freezing cold. He could handle it for a long period of time. Cade knew Dean couldn't. Except Dean's unwillingness to even work with him to piece it together was killing him.

He tried to close the gap and Dean skipped a step backward. The move sliced Cade through, chilling him in ways the winter temperatures couldn't come near.

"Just go home, Cade. Call me when you figure out which lie you're going to fix first. Or better yet, don't bother." He shifted his glare from him to the bar. "It seems awful convenient, now. I meet you, you do a good night's favor and suddenly my bar gets torched like a bad bonfire."

"I wasn't any part of this," he argued, his apprehension swinging quickly to anger of his own. He had no idea where the idea for blame came from.

Narrowed eyes focused on him. "But you're here now. Why? What are you hiding?"

"I told you—"

"*Riiight*, because everyone likes to walk around in the freezing cold, half-naked, at night. Searching for what?"

"Fuck you," he growled lowly. "If you'd let me explain—" As soon as he spoke, he realized his mistake.

Dean spun on a heel and stalked away. He was around the corner in two strides and gone. A few seconds later, Cade heard the smack of the car door and the shriek of the car's motor being brought to life.

Headlights flooded the area then the car was on the road and gaining speed. Leaving him behind.

Dean punched the side of the shed, rocking it on its foundation. Not one of his best moments.

"Damn it." Icy air filled his lungs as he fought to calm himself.

No. He'd made the first move. He wasn't letting him stomp away. If Dean wanted the full truth, wanted answers, then Cade was going to give them to him. There was no going backwards now.

Locking his helmet into place, he started his bike and rolled from behind the remains of the bar. Taillights were visible in the distance. He had a good guess they were Dean's.

Zipped into his jacket, he cranked the throttle and raced after the man.

Chapter Ten

Trailing a minute or two at the most, he pulled up behind Dean's car. The motor was still ticking as metal cooled when he marched past it. He pounded on the front door. "Dean!" Not loud enough to scare neighbors, but hopefully Dean got that he was serious.

The door whipped open. The anger was clear. The green of his eyes sparked like fireworks. "Fuck. Off."

Dean went to slam it on him but Cade shoved his foot in the way to block it. "You want the truth," he challenged. "Open this damned door."

"Which truth?" he jeered.

"About why I was there. Why I didn't answer." His voice lowered with honesty. "I'll tell you everything."

"Don't know why I'm trusting you, *again.*" Grudgingly, he widened the door opening.

"Because I haven't given you any reason not to trust me," he replied. He walked in cautiously. Dean was silently fuming. The door shut smartly.

"Fine. Talk." He crossed his arms.

"I was telling you the truth. I had hoped I could dig a little and find something overlooked. As for why I *couldn't* answer, wolves can't speak."

Dean rolled his eyes. "You. Are. Insane." He reached for the doorknob. "Goodbye."

"I'm asking again. What color were its eyes?"

"I told you — gray."

Cade grasped him by the shoulders and forced Dean to face him. "My family has a secret. Myself, Quade, and Chris. It is inherited from our father. Once a month, we gather to run. We run as a pack. Wolves."

Slow-dawning realization leeched his face of color. "That's not possible," he croaked.

"Oh, it's very possible. We just don't advertise for safety reasons. I rather like having my skin, this one and the furry one, intact. We're wolf shifters." He heaved a huge breath as he said those last three words. Something he'd never dreamed of telling another human being was finally out in the open. "It's not something we share freely."

"So that...dog..."

"Wasn't a dog," he replied calmer. "I snooped the fields, the dumpster, and had finished the storage room where you'd mentioned the rags had been stored. I'd just walked behind the bar when you pulled up. I hid until I had no choice, because you found my motorcycle."

He still held onto Dean's shoulders. The man hadn't moved beneath his hands. "I didn't want you to find out like this."

Dean blinked and edged a step away. "Fine. You can go now."

Cade didn't trust that tone. There was something...hollow in Dean's gaze. "Do you believe me?"

"Sure," he said, almost too quickly, rushed even. He avoided touching Cade as he reached for the door. "Thanks for explaining it."

Cade's hand blocked the door. "Dean?"

"What?"

"You saw the wolf. You talked to him. He knows who you are."

"Sure he does," he said, like he was addressing a child, or a mental patient.

Cade sighed. His chest ached with failure. He wasn't going to stand there all night arguing over it. "Okay, I can tell this isn't going anywhere." He pushed on the door to shut out the cold. "Can I at least use your bathroom before you kick me out?"

Dean pressed his lips together, like the request went against his better judgment. "I suppose."

"Thanks." He refrained from reaching to touch the man. Clearing the living room, he walked past the kitchen to the small bathroom in the hallway.

Once inside, he flicked on the light and started stripping. Item by item he tossed his clothes on the sink counter until he stood naked. Tugging the tie from his hair last, he dropped it in a boot.

"Okay. I hope you're ready for this," he muttered. Whether he meant Dean, his wolf, or even himself, he had no idea. He heard Dean shuffling around in the living room, probably antsy to get rid of him.

Too bad it wasn't going to happen.

He cracked the door open so the wolf could paw at it and focused. Dean's tread was distracting and loud from the other room as he merged, letting the wolf come forward.

Almost as soon as he landed on four paws, he started to growl. Noises were clearer, more distinct. Thuds and grunts. The wolf scratched at the door. A scent reached him. Tangy. Pungent. And it was Dean's. *Fear.*

Something crashed to the floor. Cade clawed to get the door open. He whipped around the doorframe to race down the hallway toward the ruckus.

Growling, he tucked his legs and launched at the person struggling with Dean. The man shouted in surprise, losing his grip. Dean fell to the ground, catching himself on his hands, gasping. He reached for his throat, visibly shaking.

Cade snapped and growled at the person in front of him, backing him up. Dean heaved and gagged, pulling Cade's attention away from his attacker for a split second.

It was all that was needed for the man to lunge for the front door and flee from the house. Cade jumped after him, trying to get a leg between his teeth, but he missed.

When Cade wanted to pursue, the wolf refused and the three or four seconds they struggled, the guy leaped into a pickup truck and spun tires to get away.

Cade cursed, shaking the wolf, but he wouldn't be swayed. Dean had been hurt. Mates first.

A last look proved the vehicle was gone anyway. *Going to have a long talk about that,* he warned. The wolf trotted back to the house like it owned the world.

Cautiously, he cleared the steps and peeked into the living room through the gaping doorway. A lamp had been knocked over, creating an odd halo of light, but it was still on, brightening the room. Dean was resting on his calves, breathing easier.

When his gaze landed on the wolf poking its head into the house, his breath hitched, clicked, and stopped. His eyes grew wide.

The wolf, of course, obeyed *now* when he instructed it to shut the door. Inside, Cade rolled his eyes with exasperation. With shoves of its nose, he nudged at the door until it clicked.

"What the hell," Dean croaked. "Cade!" He twisted to call over his shoulder without losing his focus on the wolf. "Cade. Man, this isn't the time for bullshit."

The wolf sat. Cade didn't try to get closer. Faced with the truth, Cade had to be patient. At least now he couldn't argue or deny. Not when Cade sat five feet in front of him.

He watched as Dean cautiously rose to his feet, wobbling a little. "Cade, seriously, asshole. Did you go to China to piss?"

The wolf chuffed with laughter. Cade hated making him nervous again, but sometimes reality had to be faced head on. And after this, it was clear someone had a target on Dean. He had faith that truck and driver was the same one responsible for the ripped out stud at the bar. No way in hell was he going to walk out that door now.

With stuttered steps, Dean moved further away, into the kitchen and then the hall. He never let his gaze stray from Cade until he was out of sight.

"Uh, Cade," he tried again. "What the—? Son of a bitch." Dean reappeared moments later carrying all of his clothes, even his boots. "So this is what took you so long to begin with?"

The wolf nodded with Cade's answer.

Dean's eyes closed briefly and he sank to his knees on the floor. The pile of clothing tumbled from limp fingers. Shock dulled the color of his eyes when he gazed at Cade. "You can understand me?"

The wolf's head bobbed again.

"What just happened?" he asked.

Cade couldn't answer, so he did what he could to get answers. He snuffled on the ground where the man had fallen and found his scent in the carpet. He trailed it first to the master bedroom, a door that now stood open, then backtracked down the hall to the rear door.

The mechanism had been popped. The metal framework around the door was bent out of place. He trotted to Dean and nudged him gently at his elbow. He wanted his clothes but guessed they'd get to that point soon. He was positive Dean wasn't ready to see the transition happen.

"I can't believe this," Dean muttered, but found his feet and followed him down the hall. "Fucking shit!" He smacked the wall by the rear door when he spotted what Cade had found. "I have to call the police. You better—" He waved a hand in the air. "I sure as hell can't explain a wolf."

Dean didn't so much as look at him as he cleared the living room for his bedroom, shutting the door between.

Whether it was for Cade's privacy or Dean's mental state to calm, he didn't hesitate. Clothes were going to be a necessity to be questioned by the cops.

* * * *

Dean fell over backward onto his bed. When did his life take a sharp left into fantasyland? There was a *motherfucking wolf* in his living room. Okay, maybe not *now*. Now, there would only be Cade. He shuddered, still fighting the obvious with the unreality of it.

A light tap on his bedroom door not too long after pulled him out of his crossed thoughts.

"Can I come in?"

"Sure," he answered.

Cade sat on the edge of the bed, but didn't touch. "I'm sorry for springing it on you like that," he said. "If I'd left, you'd never agree to see me again."

Dean grunted.

"Did you see who it was? I didn't get a real good look."

"I think I've seen him at the bar," he offered. Hell. He had no idea. "Someone broke into my house and tried to kill me."

The ghosting feel of fingertips brushed over his throat. "Are you okay?"

"It feels bruised. He had something. A wire. What do they call them? A garrote?"

"That's what it looks like. It's raw but it didn't break the skin."

He opened tired eyes. "Thank you. What does that make now? Three times?"

"Twice. Tossing out drunk trash doesn't count."

Dean snorted and Cade's lips twitched. "I don't want to call the police. I want to be numb."

"I know, but this is serious. Someone is out for you."

Dean gazed at the man. *Gray eyes.* Now he saw it clearly. No wonder the wolf had stood outside of the bar for so long. There was no mistaking them now. He knew that gaze, and well. Right now it was filled with concern.

He raised a hand to touch the side of Cade's face. "Why do your eyes stay the same?" He wasn't ready to think about why someone wanted him dead. He couldn't go there. Not yet.

So was it any saner that he wanted to talk about Cade's ability to *change into a damned wolf*? He had no idea.

"Dad tried to explain it once. Babies are born with nearly fully grown, but not developed, eyesight. That's why the irises always look so huge for infants. It's a sensory tool that wouldn't take the change without adverse repercussions. We don't lose a lot of our vision, some color, but everything else is enhanced. Scent, hearing. We also heal faster and cleaner. The change isn't exactly painless but it becomes second nature, and it happens so fast, we really stop noticing."

"That is remarkable. All three of you?"

Cade smiled, a lot kinder now. "Yeah. We're all animals."

Dean chuckled. His eyelids drooped. Life was just weird.

"Feeling calmer now?"

"Yeah. Just shook up. Maybe Kelly or whoever they send out will be able to get prints off the back door."

"At least it doesn't look like he wanted to rob you while he was at it. Who knows how long he was here."

Dean rolled his head on the bed to study his surroundings. The room looked untouched. Small favors.

"What did I do? Who did I do it to?" he mumbled. "I haven't really spoken to anyone since Daniel died. The people I was friends with have drifted away. There's Garret, but he worked for me. He has a wife and a baby. He wouldn't do something like this." He frowned, cupping his throat. "He wouldn't do something like *this*, either."

"You said it looked like someone from the bar. A regular?"

"I'm not sure. I only saw him when he was on the ground avoiding teeth."

"Heh." Cade sounded pleased with that description.

Dean hefted up onto propped elbows. "Might as well get this over with."

Cade stood and offered a hand. "We better get the logistics right before they get here. A wolf chasing him out of the house isn't going to fly."

"No, but a large biker dude with size sixteen boots sure will."

"They're fourteen, thank you," he groused.

Dean jostled him, laughing roughly.

Dean phoned the police while Cade also made a call. "I need to get someone to do the PM checks. I'm not leaving tonight," he explained when he was done.

Dean frowned, but didn't argue. He doubted his asshole home invader would return tonight. Trying to swallow reminded him exactly why Cade staying really wasn't such a bad idea.

It took a while after making the call before a cruiser pulled up, making Dean antsy. He didn't relax until Officer Archer and his sidekick knocked.

Reports were taken as well as pictures of the bruising around Dean's throat. He stayed out of the way while Officer Saucedo did the fingerprint search around the door.

"Are you in the system?" he asked Dean when he was finished. Kelly was currently picking at Cade for his side of the story.

"As far as I know," Dean replied. "I had to fingerprint for the county to get the bar's licensing."

Saucedo nodded. "I'll double check what I've got and let you know if any of the lifts match or not."

Dean smiled weakly. "Thanks."

"Did he touch the back door at all?" He waved his pen toward Cade. Saucedo was writing down notes on a notepad as Dean spoke.

"No. He used the restroom. We both guessed the guy who did this thought he'd left and that was when he attacked."

Kelly was talking to Cade, taking the same kind of report details. Dean slid a look in their direction, but either Cade was focused, or was simply avoiding looking his way. He didn't meet Dean's searching.

"Are you two in a relationship?"

It was asked in a matter-of-fact way, but it still managed to tongue-tie Dean. *Were they?* "Yeah, I guess we are."

The other man nodded.

"It seems he's been around when this stuff has been happening."

Dean narrowed his eyes at the insinuation. "He helped one night at the bar, and became a friend. I've met his family. They're good people. He has nothing to do with what's been happening."

Cool eyes met his.

That insolence only fueled Dean's anger. "And if you check your records, he was on call for the Rose Vet Clinic in Silo the morning the bar burned."

"Just covering bases, Mr. Eckler."

"Well, leave Cade out of it. Considering how shorthanded you boys have been this winter, I'd rather have him at my back than having to rely on someone thirty minutes across town. If it had come to waiting for you, I'd be dead."

Saucedo's checks flushed red. He knew he'd scored in pointing out that fact.

"Just see if you can actually find the person behind this, because I'm beginning to think it's the same guy for all of these attacks, including the fire. Cade saw him get into a truck before he could catch up to him. A truck was used to bring down the roof. Odds are it's the same lunatic who torched Gemini's!" His voice had begun to rise with growled anger.

Someone was trying to kill him and the Cassan cops were acting like the Keystone cops!

"Easy." Cade's calming voice rushed into his ear.

Dean closed his eyes and sucked hard, deep breaths. A strong arm wound around his waist. Dean hadn't heard him come closer. He didn't care if it made either of the two cops uncomfortable, he leaned into Cade's strength. He was tired. The shock was getting to him. As if he needed one more thing today.

"If you remember any other details, don't hesitate to call," Sheriff Archer was saying. "I'll see if I can narrow the vehicle search with these details and what's already on record."

"Thank you," Cade replied.

"And I'll let you know if I can find a connection to Daniel's death in this. Give me a day or two to review the files."

"If we have a day or two. So far, this has been random, but it's clear he's been following Dean enough to know where he's going to be and where he lives."

The arm holding him tightened as he listened to Cade.

"And whether it started out as attempted murder or not, it's pretty clear that is his intent now."

"I understand the worry." Kelly frowned. "I've known Dean since both he and Daniel moved to Cassan. It's not right that you're being targeted after what happened to Daniel."

"I appreciate you handling it, Kelly." He knew it had to be bringing up memories for the man. He was handling it like the professional Dean had always known him to be.

Both officers left a few minutes later, the cop cruisers turning around and disappearing.

"What did he mean by that?"

"He and Daniel were starting to get close when he died. Kelly is gay, but refuses to live it out in the open. He's the law and Cassan may be a nice town, but it's not all that open."

"Do you think that has something to do with all of this?"

He shrugged. "I've mentioned it to him," Dean replied. "I don't hide who I am. I've never been in the closet. It's all Kelly knows."

"That is a rough way to live."

Dean pressed into Cade's chest. There was understanding in his voice. He didn't argue when Cade looped arms and tugged him chest to chest. He was exhausted, drained, and out of *oh shit*s when it came to being shocked.

"How's your throat?"

"Sore."

Dean didn't protest when Cade simply took charge and took care of him.

Chapter Eleven

Cade shooed Dean off to the shower while he figured out something to make to eat. Dean wasn't sure what he'd come up with but wasn't going to complain. The evening had been one shock after another following hard on the heels of a sit on his thumbs day. A slow, hot shower would help unwind his nerves. At least he hoped so.

Drying off then dressing in clean jeans and a light sweatshirt, he emerged and was instantly hit with the smell of warm maple syrup, pancakes, and eggs. *Breakfast for dinner?* Worked for him.

"God, that smells good." He curled his arms around Cade's middle. Dean pressed a cheek between shoulder blades, savoring the strength he held.

"I hope it's okay. At least it's soft stuff."

"It'll be fine." He nuzzled close. "Thank you."

Cade rubbed over Dean's knuckles resting at his waist. "Any time."

Dean reluctantly released him to pull plates from the cabinet. Once they were settled, they ate in calm silence at the table. Cade had left his hair untied after... Well, after the whole wolf thing.

It wasn't a facet of his day he was willing to focus on yet. Soon, but not right then. He didn't have the fortitude to break down everything he'd seen tonight. Not at the bar. Not in his living room.

Dean blinked when he realized he was staring blankly across the table. What caught his eye? Cade had swept a swath of hair over his shoulder. The move made Dean's fingers itch to feel its warmth. This was twice Cade had been with him and he'd left his hair loose. He hid his smile, wondering if he'd done it on purpose. He couldn't help that he was drawn to it.

Cade gave him a hand in cleaning up afterward, asking, "Do you mind if I take a shower?"

"Help yourself." He waved toward his bedroom. It was pretty clear to him that Cade would be sharing his bed.

"Thanks."

Dean watched him pad across the rooms until he was out of sight. A few minutes later, the rush of water could be heard through the house pipes. Done with the dishes, he checked the thermostat for the night and locked the doors, making sure the back door was secure. He frowned while running a finger over the damaged metal of the frame. He'd unearth his tools in the morning and fix it. The house wasn't much but it was all he had. All he needed really.

With that done for the night, he went to the bedroom. It felt odd having someone in the bathroom. Even when he'd lived with Daniel, they'd had a two bedroom apartment. Shared the bathroom, but they'd been sharing since they were babies. This felt different.

He kicked back on the bed and crossed his ankles, his hands on his stomach. His eyes drifted shut and he relaxed. The sounds of Cade moving around lulled him. It had been a while since he'd had a boyfriend. The fact that Cade wanted to be there for him hit a spot inside that was hungry for the attention. *Possibly more? Affection?* He had no idea.

Cade was so new to all of this. Dean didn't want to hang his hat on this as a sure thing, not yet, anyway.

The bed dipped at his thigh as Cade slid in next to him. "I found a toothbrush in the cabinet. I slobbered all over it, so I guess it's mine now."

Dean chuckled. "Sure. I forgot to tell you they were there." He lifted heavy eyelids and landed his gaze on the hunk of goodness lying beside him. Toweled damp hair flowed over his shoulder. "You're more redhead than Chris. I hadn't noticed."

"It comes out when it's wet. Somewhere in the family tree stuff," he teased warmly. He threaded fingers through the strands. "I don't know why, I've always liked it long."

"I won't complain," he assured him. "I happen to have a thing for longer hair."

Pleasure sparkled in his gaze. "Lucky me," he said with a breathy tease.

Dean slithered down to lay flat on the bed. "You have no idea." He reached with a hand and caressed Cade's bare chest, stroking the light strands of hair beneath learning fingertips. The man wore underwear, a sexy pair of hip hugging, short cut underwear, and nothing else. His ribs flexed with each breath. It was no secret how much he turned Dean on.

Lying close together, body heat rolled over Dean in waves. The cautious touch of fingers to his neck stilled him. Not out of fear. He could see Cade's worry in his expression.

"I'm fine," he whispered, able to read his thoughts plainly.

"What if I'd actually left?" he asked.

"Don't play that game. You didn't." He captured the wandering hand and curled it into his palm. "I'll be careful until they get this guy. I don't plan on being caught like that again. I'd like to kick his ass myself."

Cade smirked.

"Hey, just because you've never seen it, don't think I can't."

"Wasn't saying anything."

"Uh huh." Dean wasn't buying his innocent act. He'd already guessed Cade was the *manly man* type of guy. That didn't bother him, so long as he didn't forget Dean was too. Daniel had been the gentler of the two boys.

After a drawn out silence, surprisingly, maybe, Cade was the one to make the first move. He lowered to find Dean's lips, brushing over them with light strokes, testing. Dean's heart jolted into a new speed.

Wanting. He was drowning in it. He grasped at Cade's hair, fisting it into his palm, tugging as yearning boiled higher.

A low growl slipped from Cade and the hesitancy of his kiss vanished. Broad shoulders pinned him. Hard chest met hard chest. Dean's free hand glided down Cade's side, gripping flesh when he could reach no further.

Cade's hips ground into him in answer, digging his hardening length into Dean's thigh. Dean kissed him through the confusion as Cade's body came alive for him. There were stutters, a few gasps. Shocks. Sensations he'd never experienced. Dean was flying being the one to give that to him.

Wiggling beneath his hard frame, he pressed upward and urged Cade to roll to his back. Cade relented, breaking their kiss with a gust of air.

"Is there anything you don't like?" Dean nibbled on his jaw, letting him know he wasn't going to rush anything.

"Not like?"

"Or are super sensitive to?"

Cade blinked, his brain clearly not being overly helpful in filling in blanks. "I— I don't think so. So much already feels different."

Dean slowed, hefting up on braced arms to stare into wide eyes. "Different?"

"Not bad. I'd tell you if it were."

Dean nodded once. "Good." He was glad to hear that.

Cade's palm captured him from behind and tugged him down for more of those deep kisses.

Dean obliged, centering himself above Cade, nestling neatly between his thighs. He groaned. Now *here*, here he could die a happy man. With nothing but two layers of thin cotton underwear between them, heat scorched. Nerves sparked, making cocks pulse. His skin felt alive, tightening with need.

"Oh, man," he groaned, rocking slowly. His eyes sank shut as sensation rushed through him. He wasn't sure how much longer he'd even be able to string coherent thoughts together. He pushed down, heat building between them.

Cade's hands delved beneath elastic. Dean's thrust stuttered until Cade's insistence got him moving again. Cade wasn't being hesitant in exploring his desires or what he could find beneath his palms. Broad hands left no misunderstanding, gripping firmly to keep Dean moving.

Dean found his lips, claiming them as desires flared brighter. Harsh breathing filled the quiet of the bedroom.

When Cade nudged at his underwear, Dean didn't argue. He arched his rear and Cade rolled them down his hips. Dean worked them lower until he could kick them free. Hooking Cade's in his fingers, he did the same for him, ripping them away. They joined Dean's on the floor.

Something needy and seductive swirled in Cade's gaze sucking in Dean when he climbed onto the bed.

Dean wasn't going to baby the man, questioning every little action. He trusted Cade to know his own limits, and to say something if Dean was pushing him for more than he was ready for.

He had nothing to worry about. Hovering over him, before he could decide between laving his chest or going right for his mouth, Cade made the decision for him. He yanked Cade straight down, wrapping a single leg over the back of Dean's thigh.

Cade's groan was sheer hunger. Need.

Then Dean was being kissed senseless. Strong hands never stopped touching, grasping, caressing.

Braced above him on elbows, he returned the kisses, devouring Cade as ferociously. It seemed to be exactly what the man wanted. Grunts and growls escaped on panted breaths. Dean started rocking again. His body knew what it wanted, knew what he craved. Flesh to flesh. Every contact shot lust-filled surges over nerves and muscle, clenching and grinding to meet Cade's movements.

Everything he needed was packed into Cade's hard frame. Rubbing dick to dick, they challenged each other, strived for more. Weeping fluids from both eased the strokes until Dean was gliding seamlessly against skin.

Dean groaned Cade's name when he broke from the kisses. Cade cupped his ass, bringing him closer, harder. His eyes glittered, pinned on Dean.

Dean knew that look and he wasn't going to taunt either of them, not their first time. He needed this as much as Cade.

Flexing his hips, his aching length was captured between their slicked bodies. The need to come launched through his system, racing through veins. Cade was waiting for him, watching him.

Dean gasped when a twitch of pressure near his entrance added to the growing fire in his blood.

"You want me there, don't you?" Cade's voice rumbled.

Dean nodded.

"Picture it. Me taking you."

Dean did. He thrust harder in reaction. Every muscle locked up as he spurted between them unable to stop the rush. Liquid heat pooled between his and Cade's abdomens.

Cade shuddered. Pressing into the pillow to arch his body into Dean's, he followed, adding to the spunk. His throbbing shaft pressed into skin as he found his release, making Dean moan.

Panting, Dean sank close. He tucked against Cade's shoulder, each trying to catch their breaths. A thumb stroked in circles over a butt cheek where Cade lightly held him. Dean sighed. He wasn't one for pillow talk, but he loved after sex cuddles. He supposed it could be called a weakness but he honestly didn't care.

"That was okay?"

Dean smiled and kissed Cade's throat below his ear. "It gets even better."

"You keep saying that," Cade pointed out.

"Have I been wrong?"

Cade twisted on the pillow to find his lips for a brief kiss. "No."

"Then don't sweat the small shit." He hefted up onto his palms, his gaze landing on Cade's flushed face. Sharp pants were slowing. "Let's get cleaned up."

"I have to get up early. Still on at the vet clinic."

"I'll set the clock."

Cade followed him to the restroom, both washing up at the sink. Dean spotted his furrowed brow in the mirror's reflection. He hoped the man wasn't regretting what they'd shared. He'd seemed fully on board at the time.

"Don't go cold on me again, Cade," he warned.

"What?"

"You're frowning."

Cade raised his chin, his features smoothing some. "Not over this. Not about what just happened." He threaded the towel on the hanging bar to air out.

Dean caught the light as they both sauntered to the bed. When Cade didn't bother with his underwear, Dean followed suit. So he was a bare skin sleeper. Like Dean would complain about sleeping next to his naked body?

"So if it wasn't this…" He left it out there, waiting for Cade to fill in the blanks.

"I don't like the idea of you being here alone."

Dean studied the man. On one side of the coin, that was a nice thought. It made him think that maybe this could be more for Cade, eventually. That he was thinking about Dean for more than sex.

The other side of the coin wasn't as pleased with the implication that Dean couldn't handle himself alone.

"Cade…" He stressed it with a disgruntled sigh. He set the clock for the other man with a quick check of time.

"I know. It's partially me, and partially the wolf. It's his ingrained survival instincts to be close to—" He bit it off. "To be close. I'll leave it at that for now." He sank down onto the bed and Dean copied him, tugging up blankets.

"So there's like two voices pushing at you?"

"Yeah, I guess so." He stretched out an arm in invitation. "Humor me, okay?" he added when Dean balked. "I know you're not a woman. I like to hold."

That was exactly what Dean wanted to hear. He softened his reaction with a smile. "I'm good with that."

"I'm not trying to challenge you being a man. Adjustments are going to take time. I'm not doing anything to undermine who you are. I'm simply doing what feels right, being me."

Dean nodded, stretched along his side. "That's all I can ask." When quiet filled the room, he wondered what else the man was thinking. Dean could tell he wasn't asleep. "Just spit it out. I'm not going to kick you out of bed."

Cade grunted low in his throat. "You haven't said anything about how you feel about the wolf."

Dean felt his tension, heard the trepidation mingled in his words. They were touching in several places with Dean draped down his side resting on

Cade's shoulder. This close, there was nothing Cade could hide from Dean.

"I'm not sure yet, to be honest."

Cade took his time before asking, "Does it scare you?"

"The animal itself? No." A slow rise and fall of Cade's chest revealed more than he was saying. Hard muscles relaxed in waves a heartbeat at a time. "You said it was inherited from your father." Cade nodded. "Can you pass it on?"

"Any of us can. It's a sub-gene, I guess. It looks like anything else in a DNA test, but it's not. I'm not even sure that's a right description."

"It's camouflaged? Like a chameleon?"

Cade hummed in thoughtful musing. "Yeah. Never looked at it that way. That's probably why only men can pass the gene. Women have the ability to take on the wolf but can't pass it on."

"So it doesn't fall within the female chromosome chain. I can see why you don't want science or anyone finding out about you guys. You'd be one heck of tool to exploit."

Cade sighed. "Yeah. We have to be careful. As a pack, we protect our own."

"As a pack... So, Jamie and Chris?"

"Are part of the pack. Quade and Maya, too. Well, she will be. I doubt he'll fail with her. She's smart. Fear can only survive when there is ignorance. She's far from that."

"I got that, too." Dean laughed ruefully. "I think he's got a handful, woman or not. She's a natural redhead."

Cade grinned, joining him in the humor. "Poor bro." They snickered in unison.

136

Dean found strands of hair and twirled it around his fingers. "If the wolf doesn't scare me," he said thoughtfully, "and I happen to really like the guy he's a part of..." He watched Cade's facial expressions where he stared upward at the ceiling. "I mean, how can I be upset or scared by an animal that stopped a murderer? One of these days, I want to see you...change? Is that what you do?"

"Pretty much."

He played with the hair he held for a few minutes. "I'm coming to terms with it," he finally admitted. "I'm also making a stab in the dark that this is a very elite, private type of club."

"Very private. But it's twofold. While you protect us, and our secret, we protect those in the pack."

"Pack?"

Cade rolled his head a little on the pillow to meet his stare. "Why don't we leave it there for tonight? We have time."

"All right." Dean curled up closer a moment later and Cade wrapped him fully into his side. He waited as the tension that had been building in Cade's frame gradually lessened. He had to assume there were things either Cade wasn't ready to share, or that he felt would be too much for Dean to handle, one shock on top of another, after another. This *had* been one of the oddest days of his life.

He'd been face to face with the wolf and never once had it acted threatening toward Dean. The wolf was a part of Cade, from what he could understand. The animal had responded when he'd spoken to it, so there was some facet of Cade that existed within the animal when he was wolf. Not even the smartest dog could comprehend questions or conversation to answer with human-like gestures. To Dean, it came down to they were one and the same.

He replayed frames of the animal, of its behavior, of its attack on the other man. Dean realized the wolf had made sure to only go after the man struggling with Dean. Was that what Cade meant in protecting their own? He had a feeling it wasn't that simple, and it wasn't the end of the conversation.

Dean's gaze flowed over Cade's resting profile while his mind churned with all the new information. Gray eyes had finally closed in sleep. It took him a little longer for his brain to stop dissecting the day's events, but he eventually managed to do the same.

Chapter Twelve

Cade rolled into the pillow, his arm weighted down at the shoulder. He sniffed and snuffled at the hair tickling his chin, then sighed, floating toward consciousness, in no hurry to get out of the warm bed. His entire world had been upended a little more than a month ago. He still didn't have a firm grip on all of the changes. The only thing he did know was he had to keep Dean safe. Nothing more had happened since the attack on Dean in his home several days before. Cade hadn't been able to sleep in his own bed without him because of that need, because of the threat to Dean.

The other conundrum he faced was taking a little longer to come to terms with. He didn't know if it meant he'd lost the battle to the wolf or not, or if he'd really been hiding his whole life from something that should be natural now. He honestly didn't know.

He'd had girlfriends. Cade had always appreciated them, had never felt like he was forcing something to be with them, to enjoy their company. He and Quade had double-dated too many times to count. The novelty of dating twins, he supposed. Had that been a smokescreen, a copout? He honestly didn't know.

There was an intensity between him and Dean that he'd never known, even with all the women he had dated. Was that more of the mating bond? He knew he simply needed to accept. Cade did like the man. Only it wasn't as *simple* as that. Or was it? His mind continued to tumble.

Was *like* enough to build on? To be the beginning point of the rest of their lives?

He swallowed slowly. That fact hit him with blinding reality. This was it. Dean was the one person he was fated to be with, to spend the rest of his life with.

Not doubting Chris but needing a second opinion, he'd checked the wolf's error percentage within their pack and any others he could ask their alpha about. His brother hadn't been wrong. The wolf never erred.

Cade was fighting the inevitable even though he liked Dean, enjoyed being with him. And the sex? He stifled the electric shiver. Dean brought something out in Cade that was pure need. Possession. Hunger. A tenderness that burned bright to his very soul. He wanted to do things, be inside him, surround the other man. If it was only the pure sexual hunger driving him, he could accept that, but it was more, and that was what terrified him.

Was he supposed to...*love*...him? Cade jumped away from the possibility as though he stood at the edge of a sharp cliff. Love a man? He wasn't sure of any feelings, right then.

He'd cared for Laura. They'd dated, had hot and heated sex, he'd met her parents. The next step had seemed unquestionable... But he'd known even then she wasn't the wolf's mate, so he'd ended it feeling he was doing both of them wrong. He was keeping her from finding someone who could really love her and make her happy, and Cade had thought his mate was not far into his future. Well, apparently only a few years into his future.

He sniffed again. Musk and body-heated cotton. Scents that he was beginning to recognize as Dean. Warmth suffused his chest. *Mate.* Not Laura. Not pack. Not even female. Maybe the time and distance since dating her was to his benefit. Would he have become friends with Dean, open to more, if he'd ended a relationship recently before meeting him? Would he have been as willing to help? Or to listen to his wolf? Or believe this was possible? Children really did seem like such a small hurdle now.

Dean's cell phone rang on the nightstand. Neither moved. Cade knew it was Dean's mother by the tone. Dean always called her back, but he didn't necessarily jump when she called. Cade supposed he understood, since she still called daily. Mothers worried. It was simple fact.

Dean stretched alongside him disturbed by the call nonetheless, muscles flexing followed by a slow exhale. The motions brushing them skin to skin disrupted Cade's tumultuous thoughts easily.

Cade lowered his chin to nuzzle at Dean's nape where his hair had fallen to expose him. It was becoming so easy to touch, to give in to the wanting. Another sign that this was right between them? Was there any other way to look at it? He didn't know. He did know he liked doing it, liked the way he felt, liked the way Dean responded.

Especially liked the way Dean reacted. Like it all felt good for him. Like he wanted more. As if his nudging and pushing into Cade weren't clear enough. Cade had to admit these changes would be so much harder to accept if he not only had to convince himself, but had to win over Dean at the same time. He would have fought the attraction a lot harder if Dean had been indifferent, but the fact that he wasn't made Cade's cravings rise to the surface in answer.

Dean voiced a small rumble as Cade drifted his lips over his nape to a bare shoulder. He didn't sleep in a shirt, even in the dead of winter. Cade was liking that fact right then.

Curling him close within his arms, he glided against Dean's body. His cock eased playfully against firm ass cheeks, finding a warm haven hinted at beneath the underwear.

"Morning," Dean rasped.

Cade murmured something, his lips too occupied for an actual verbal reply.

Dean began to undulate into Cade's chest, rocking his hips in earnest against the press of Cade's desire. His sighs turned into aroused moans. He reached for one of Cade's hands and together, they wiggled under elastic and encircled Dean's very hard dick. Both shuddered. Steel hard and throbbing. Cade stroked him slowly. Seemed he wasn't the only one *awake* this morning. He growled in appreciation.

Without thinking about the whys, he had to have Dean naked. He had to feel all that hot skin against his own. He pushed at Dean's underwear and he got the message, lifting and arching to glide them off.

Cade tossed the blankets away and urged Dean to his chest. Any noticeable change of temperature was utterly unimportant. Smooth skin slipped under his palm, warmed from sleep.

Dean moaned when Cade added a little pressure to his fingertips, roaming over muscle.

"That feels so good," he said in appreciation, muffled by the pillow.

"I want you," Cade managed through a dry mouth. His heart pounded with the resounding echo of an anvil into his ribs.

Dean stretched an arm for the bedside stand, tugging on the drawer. "In there."

Cade rose up on his knees and found lube and condoms. His hand shook only a little when he released them to land on the bed at Dean's hip. This wasn't any kind of a small step for him, for them.

Settling, he straddled Dean's thighs. Firm and slightly round with dimples. Dean's butt flexed, making Cade grin gently. He leaned forward and bit at a side, getting a soft yelp from Dean, followed by a rough chuckle. "Bastard."

"Did I hurt you?"

"Just surprised me." He remained relaxed, splayed on the mattress. Cade could see his smile grow bolder. "Do it again."

Cade did, willingly nipping, biting, and licking, until Dean was writhing beneath his weight. The man panted, his fingers clawed into the sheets when he stopped.

He breathed out Cade's name in a growl. The hungry sound fired need into Cade's blood.

"Turn over."

He made room for Dean to flip. The bed rocked with his jostling, harried breathing loud as he settled. A raised hand trailed through Cade's loose hair. Dean's fascination with it amused Cade.

When Dean slipped free, Cade moved from the bed and dropped his underwear. Returning, he stretched out along Dean's side where he shifted, widening his legs. Cade couldn't ignore that. He cupped Dean's sac, hearing a heated hiss of pleasure being forced through his teeth.

"Yeah?"

"Fuck...yeah," he ground out.

Cade slid from the hardening globes in his palm to Dean's cock, roaming as he learned. He pumped and Dean moaned, dropping into a whine for more.

Cade wasn't going to disappoint him.

Squeezing the tube, he coated his fingers. Leaning close, he brushed over Dean's rosette and the man flexed, arching, reaching. "More?"

"Yeah," he panted.

Cade teased at skin until he eased inside and he swore Dean pushed back. Gliding slowly, he felt the tightness begin to give, muscle loosening. He was right when he heard, "Another. Not going to break."

He didn't want to rush, but knew Dean was coiling tighter and tighter. His cock had softened slightly. Letting him know he wasn't going to ignore any part of him, he leaned close and licked at the tip.

"Awfuck!" He trembled, a fresh wave of sensation and blood rushing to engorge his length once more.

Cade licked his lips, discovering the taste, the salty-bitter essence. It shocked him maybe a little more than he was expecting that he liked it. He lowered again, taking the full tip between his lips and sucked lightly. He started a slow rhythm, rolling and gliding his fingers in unison with the licks and flicks of his tongue.

Fingers dug into Cade's hair, gripping him. In answer, he took more of Dean into his mouth and the man cried out. "Cade!"

Soon Dean was tugging on his hair. "Stop. Not without you inside me."

Cade relinquished his oral hold and kissed Dean's hip. It took only a moment or two to cover himself and add more lube. "Anything I should know?"

Dean opened his eyes, hunting until he landed on Cade. "Don't rush. Been a while," he replied, a graveled breathlessness to his voice. Then Dean hefted a leg behind the knee.

Cade watched, and when Dean nodded he moved closer. "Like this?"

"Trust me," he offered, filled with patience and tenderness.

Cade knew he did. If he knew nothing else, he knew that. Gripping Dean's hip and thigh, he inched closer. Wet skin pulsed. So it looked different. He lifted his chin to find Dean watching him. Without losing that gaze, he moved forward, pressing for entry until he slipped within. He gasped. "Shit," he managed in sheer shock.

"Yeah?"

"Tight."

"It gets better," Dean said.

Cade chuckled roughly, engulfed in sizzling sparks as he advanced, one slow stroke at a time. Velvet heat. Tight and all-consuming. He stilled, absorbing the differences, letting them coat his nerves until they sung in praise.

He'd never imagined it, and now he knew he couldn't live without it, without the man watching him with a fire in his eyes that seared Cade.

Slowly he began to move, encouraged by Dean's groans and beckoning body.

"That's it," Dean hissed through clenched teeth.

Cade felt the heat of skin when he caught his balls against Dean's ass. He had never filled another so completely. A shudder struck realizing that Dean was so deeply connected to him, that Cade was so deeply connected to Dean.

In that instant he accepted that it wasn't whether or not he was gay, but that Dean was the right person, the right soul, the right everything he'd been hungering for, that his wolf had been needing.

"Come on, babe," Dean prodded. "Don't lose me now."

Cade blinked. He hadn't realized he'd gone so deep into his own head, racing through his thoughts. "I'm right here," he replied. "Never losing you now." Dean's gaze glowed at those words.

Cade gripped at Dean's frame and rocked his hips. Dean grunted, his eyes falling shut. Watching the man on the bed, Cade filled him over and over, the slap of skin growing sharper, the scent of their combined bodies flooding his senses. Dean's skin had darkened from his throat to his chest with his exertions and passion. Boldly maybe, Cade accepted he'd found the most erotic visual in his lifetime.

And he was Cade's

He grunted as heat flared from his nape downward. Almost as though Dean knew him inside and out, he stroked his length, tugging as Cade spiraled closer and closer toward his orgasm.

"Fuck," he choked, his lungs aching. His body and brain had disengaged. It was sheer pleasure now.

"Yeah, yeah…" Dean groaned, clutching at the bed for leverage while he stroked himself off.

Dean arched and Cade slid home like they'd had sex a thousand times already. "Do it," he growled. He needed to feel it, see it, smell it. His wolf was panting, snarling in need. *Mate.* Cade was on the edge, the velvet heat holding him like nothing else.

Dean hooked his free leg around Cade. Mere seconds later, his mouth fell open in a silent cry as streams shot like geyser spray from the tip of his dick.

"Oh, fuck!" Cade lost it. Nerves snapped and sparked as he pulsed, rushing to fill the condom.

He stilled, drowning in the rush of endorphins. His lashes fluttered low and he stopped breathing, his heart pounding into his ribs as he floated through the burst.

In increments, the world nudged at his thoughts. Sounds, lights, scents. Dean's legs sank to the bed. Cade caressed him as he loosened the vise-like grip he'd held on his waist. He sank forward, nipping and licking at sweat dampened skin.

He didn't know he wanted it, hadn't thought this far ahead, but his mind was gone. His body was Dean's. Dragging teeth and lips over his pectoral muscle he found the thundering of Dean's heart beneath.

And bit.

Dean jerked and grunted, gripping Cade's hair. It wasn't a deep mark, and would heal. He licked over the dents in his skin, soothing them. The rest was up to Cade to deal with.

"Kinky bastard."

Cade roughly laughed. Still panting, he braced himself above Dean, pillowed on his shoulder.

"Am I off the market or something?" Dean asked humorously.

"That's one way of putting it," he replied, starting to feel his limbs again. He'd promised his life to Dean. Eventually he'd explain the full ramifications, but right now, he wanted to linger, wanted to savor.

And maybe clean up.

Without any warning, Dean suddenly started chuckling.

Cade raised onto an elbow to study him. Bright eyes sparkled upward. "I just got Chris' nickname. Fur ball." He snorted.

Cade joined him then he tapped a hip. "I guess we should get up."

Dean reached for his phone, squinting at the screen. "Mom left a message." He replaced it and rubbed a hand down his face. "Let me jump in the shower." He pushed his head deep into the pillow to meet Cade's gaze. "They're done with Gemini's. The tear down is going to start soon."

"Have you thought about what you're going to do?"

"I want to rebuild."

Cade cupped his groin, catching the condom. There were things they needed to discuss and he really didn't want to do it in his current condition. He hoped to convince Dean to move to Silo, with him. Not something to discuss right after sex, nor in their current disheveled states. He grimaced. "Let's get cleaned up. I'll make breakfast."

"You do that. You're a better cook than I am."

"Only because you don't like cooking."

Dean arched an eyebrow. "And that proves me wrong how?"

Cade chuckled and swatted at a scooting rear. He was beginning to really like that rear, too.

Chapter Thirteen

Cade worked in the kitchen, putting together something for the both of them. At least since he'd been staying around more, Dean was keeping actual food in the house. He didn't mind cooking it, if it was actually there.

Shaking the pan to rush the melting butter, he listened for the other man in the shower.

He didn't have any idea what Dean's plans were and didn't want to try to guess. This was one of those things they really needed to discuss. Cade wanted him in Silo. He *could* move to Cassan, but he'd be an hour from his brothers and the clinic. He wasn't sure how he felt about that. Except for their college years, they were never apart. They were the only family they each had, even as it appeared to be growing lately.

First Jamie, Dean and Maya, and if Duncan hung around for Ed…

A knock on the door interrupted his musings. Setting the pan on a cold burner, he ambled for the door. Expecting one of the police officers that had been around the most, he was shocked to find a woman bundled up in a coat. Standing on the step below her was, more than likely, her husband. The man was a dead ringer for Dean. Cade swallowed, slowly, as they each stared for a few seconds. By their expressions he wasn't who they'd expected either.

"Hi," she said, startled. She stared in bright confusion at Cade. She hunted over her shoulder, clearly looking for Dean's car, then faced Cade again. "I thought Dean lived here."

"He does, ma'am." He opened the door wider. "He'll be right out." They walked through the door. Was he ever glad now that he'd put on his sweatshirt and jeans. *Shii-it.* Dean's parents.

He offered a hand when he closed the door. "I'm Cade."

"Ann," she responded, slipping off a glove to shake.

He faced Dean's dad.

"Trent."

"Nice to meet you both."

They stood in awkward silence.

Cade fidgeted. "Excuse me?" He spun and aimed for the bedroom. He heard zippers and whispers. He didn't doubt for a second he was the subject of those whispers.

"Dean?" He opened the bedroom door and walked in. He found him sitting on the bed, listening to his messages.

"Crap," Dean muttered as the message played. Horror and worry darkened his gaze. "Mom—"

"Is here."

"Fuck!" he barked. "I told her not to come."

"They're both here."

He scraped a hand down a now clean-shaven face. "Shitshitshit. Why?"

"I think we both know." And Cade's gut twisted because of it. "She is going to flip when she hears everything, and sees your neck," he added quietly. It was still vivid enough to be noticeable, even days later.

Dean's palm circled his throat. His eyes shut. A few breaths helped ease the panic in his eyes.

"Let's get this over with." He stood. "Did they act funny about you?"

"Surprised."

Dean nodded absently. "Sorry. I should have told them about you before now."

"So they meet me now. Not what I would have preferred, but I'm not going anywhere, regardless." If he could, he'd stay with Dean every second until the person behind the attacks was caught. Even after, he had no intentions of leaving the man.

Cade trailed Dean from the bedroom.

"Hi, Mom. Dad."

Ann engulfed him in a hug. "Did you get my message?"

"Like two minutes ago," he replied, patting her kindly before letting her go.

"Oh, no wonder. I called two hours ago."

"I know," he grumbled good-naturedly. "Two hours ago, I was asleep. It's usual at that time of the morning. I told you you didn't have to come. There's nothing here either of you can do."

"We can be here for you," she staunchly denied. "We have a hotel room at that place outside of town, where we stayed before."

Dean let out a slow breath. "Okay." *Resigned.* Cade really felt for the man.

"Have you eaten?" Cade offered. Might as well keep going as though nothing was wrong, until something changed that.

"Just the nibbles on the flight," Dean's dad replied, taking a bit more interest in the conversation with the mention of food.

Ann scowled at her husband. It appeared she wasn't as willing to give Cade a mother's stamp of approval. Not yet.

Cade didn't take affront to her attitude. He had to pass criteria.

"Cade was making breakfast," Dean explained.

"Sounds good to me." That earned Trent another dirty look.

"I don't mind," Cade said, turning for the small kitchen. Better to get out of the direct line of fire.

"Why is his hair so long?" Cade heard the abrupt whisper.

Dean snickered. "Because he likes it that way. And so do I."

"You always were drawn to the bad boy types," she complained.

With his back turned, Cade bit his lip to not expose his laughter.

He heard Dean urge his parents to take seats in the living room. "He has tattoos, too."

Dean's mother groaned, making her son laugh. "Come on, Mom. He's a great guy. He's been sticking with me through it all since everything started."

Cade tried to not listen but the house wasn't overly large as he put together omelets and bacon. Dean regaled them of meeting Cade, the fire, meeting Cade's brothers—

"And what happened to your neck?" Trent asked with concern.

"Uh, well." He paused, and Cade heard the tension as it tightened his voice. "There have been other problems."

Cade turned down the heat on the pan and spun to rest against the counter to listen, to give Dean his support.

"Someone caused a roof collapse at Gemini's."

Ann gasped.

"Unfortunately, we were inside at the time." Cade knew he hated to admit to that part.

"Are you kidding?" Trent said, a protective firmness appearing as he sat straighter on his seat.

"No." Dean slashed a hand through his hair. "So not only is there an open arson case there's also an attempted murder investigation going on."

Ann paled. "And what does that have to do with your neck?"

Dean searched, landing on Cade with a troubled gaze. He stayed locked on Cade as he explained, "We think the same man behind the bar fire and the collapse has a vendetta or something against me."

"And you never mentioned any of this!" Ann cried. She leaped to her feet. "That's it. You're coming home. Now!"

Trent and Dean both stood. "Mom!"

"Now, Ann," Trent tried to reason.

"This is why I didn't say anything!" Dean shouted gruffly. He caught his mom by her shoulders and held her still, staring down at her pale, taut features. "I knew you would do this. I'm fine. Cade is staying here, or I'm there with him, until the guy is caught."

"I lost Daniel because of that damned bar! I'm not losing you too!"

Dean shook his head at her. She remained stiff and angry as she glared while they both fought and tugged. Finally, she acquiesced and embraced him.

"The bar isn't what got Daniel killed. You know that." He sighed, a pain-filled sound. "Daniel died trying to keep the peace, to protect the people surrounding him. I miss him, too."

Cade swallowed, stifling the rush of anguish. He would shatter if anything happened to Quade. He would never be the same. There was no comparing the depth of pain Dean lived with to anything he could possibly imagine. Cade would never be able to come close.

"I have no idea what ties all of this to the bar, other than it's been the means to hurt me the most."

Ann sniffled where she hid against Dean's shoulder. Trent stroked her back. Cade turned around to give them some privacy.

"The police are working on it. They have suspects. For all I know, that's why this happened." He lifted his chin, exposing his throat. "I'm fine, aside from the bruise and the soreness I had for a day or two."

Cade noticed he didn't attempt to explain how he managed to escape his attacker.

Dean gently steered his mother to the couch cushion where she'd been sitting with his dad. "Now, relax. Okay?"

"We still think you should come home," his mother persisted.

"I'm not coming home, not to Michigan."

"It's him, isn't it?" she nearly whispered, though Cade had no problem hearing her.

"I'll let you know," he hedged. "There's too much going on right now, so either accept it, or don't. But if you can't, then you might as well go home because I don't need the stress right now."

She huffed. Cade heard that too, even with his back turned to them.

"Fine. We are here to help."

"Then don't push at me about returning to Michigan. It's not going to happen."

Cade focused on the stove in front of him. He couldn't help the small flair of happiness Dean's words stirred. He was selfish enough to hope that he was the cause behind his refusal.

* * * *

Dean walked into the Sheriff's department that afternoon. "Hi," he said in greeting to the officer at the desk. "I got a message from Officer Archer to come talk to him."

"Let me page him." Dean was waved over to a row of seats.

A few minutes later, Kelly appeared through a heavy security door. "Dean, come on back."

Dean joined him but waited to ask anything until they were behind the door. "What's this about?"

"I have some photos I want you to look at of the guy who broke into your house."

"Do you think he's tied to the rest of it?"

Kelly looked around and lowered his voice. "I'm positive, but it's not my call." He opened a private room and let Dean enter. There were five pages, face down on the table. Once the door closed, Kelly said, "I'll tell you more after you've made a choice, or none."

Dean nodded. He pulled out a chair to get close and leaned over the table. One by one, Kelly flipped pages under the bright lights. On the fourth one, Dean's eyes widened and he raised a hand to point at the table. "Him. That's him."

"You're one hundred percent positive?"

Dean wracked his brain, flashes of the attack, of the face of the man there. "Cade could probably back me up. He didn't get a real good look, but he saw enough when he ran away." He tapped the second photo. "He's too redhead, and this guy is too old." He tapped another. "That leaves three possible." And Kelly hadn't flipped the last page yet. He studied the picture. All Dean had was the photographed face to work from, but he remembered the fleeting glimpse of the man when Cade had surprised him with his own attack. Dean had been taken by surprise, otherwise, he probably would've had a fighting chance against the man who'd been waiting for him.

He felt it in his gut. He *knew* that face even if he didn't know the man.

"What's his tie to Daniel's murder? The investigator said they had suspects. Is he one of them?" Dean searched for Kelly, who was writing on a pad.

"I need to contact the case detective. He can tell you more about that." He lowered his voice. "He's one of two in the set with the year and model of truck typical to the tire tracks we found the morning of the fire. But I didn't just tell you that."

Dean stood straight, a hand landing to rest on a chair. That did sound like good news, a good clue, or maybe just a chance to get that much closer to putting all of this behind him. "Is this all you needed?"

"For now."

He waited until he was outside by his car before calling Cade. "I'm done. I had to ID a picture."

"That's good though, right?"

"I have to hope so." It had to mean they were getting closer to what was going on and who was behind it. "What are you doing tonight?"

"Leaving it up to you. Wasn't going to assume with your parents in town."

Dean smiled. "Such a gentleman," he teased.

"Hey. Don't spread rumors."

He laughed. "Let me see what Mom and Dad are up to. She'd said something about wanting to see Gemini's before it was gone. I tried to talk her out of it." He trailed off, leaning against the car's fender. Dean knew seeing the building's carcass would be a shock for her, but she'd been insistent.

"Let her see it, and then tell her why it's important enough that you can't walk away."

There was more than the bar now, though, that he wasn't willing to walk away from. He had no idea what was going to happen between him and Cade, but he had to admit, he wanted to find out.

"Have you thought about the rebuild yet?" Cade asked.

"Some."

"Would you be willing to bring it closer to Silo?"

Dean's lips quirked up at the corner. "It's something to think about." He had a good idea he knew what Cade was hinting at. "We'll talk some more about it."

"Good," he said in breathed relief. "I'm at the clinic. I promised Quade I'd help him today, so I'll talk to you tonight."

"Okay. Call when you're free."

When Dean hung up, he called his mom next to see if they were ready to go say a final goodbye to Gemini's.

A little more than an hour later, he was rolling to a stop in front of the charred building. It looked so sad now. Burned, wrecked, and hollow.

His mother gasped as they got out of the car. "That all happened from the roof collapse?"

"Most of it." He pointed into a corner. "Some of those planks came down about four days ago. Too much snow and ice. Unfortunately, there's nothing from the inside that can be salvaged." He'd be starting from the ground up when he started over. It was kind of depressing now standing there, taking it all in.

Trent stood with his hands in his pockets, a grim frown on his features. "Have you really thought about this? Do you really want to run another bar? You have a business management degree. There must be something you can do besides this."

Dean leaned on the front of the car. There was no reason to get closer. He'd already seen enough, more times than he really wanted to count. He crossed his arms. "Honestly, I don't know. The bar was so much a part of Daniel and me."

"So why don't you come home?" his mother wheedled again. "I know you wanted to keep Gemini's after Daniel's death." She took a slow, steadying breath, her small gloved hands fisting to release at her sides. Dean knew it pained her. It would always cause her pain to think of her lost son. "But it's gone now. There's nothing left to keep you here."

Dean tucked his chin to his chest. "That's not true, Mom."

"Cade?" His mother gaped at him. "Are you serious? How long have you known him? You've never mentioned him," she accused.

"Since before Christmas." He shrugged. How was he supposed to tell his parents that until about twenty-four hours ago, what they had hadn't been serious…yet? It was still new, but he was beginning to understand what was happening between them *was happening.*

"But he's…" She waved her hands.

"Let me tell you what he is," he said with a loss of patience. "He's a damn good vet doctor. He's a supportive brother. He's been here since all of this started. He's put this whole f— this whole mess ahead of anything else in his life. He's been a good friend to me. So he has long hair, tattoos, and a motorcycle. Big deal. It doesn't make him who he is."

"And a motorcycle?" she cried.

Dean covered his eyes and rubbed with his palm. "Mom." Of course, that's what she caught in all of that.

"Mother." Trent put a hand on her shoulder and turned her around. "Let it be."

"But…" She waved a hand at the burned out shell. "This!"

"I know," Trent agreed. "And he's okay."

Dean caught his father's gaze and realized for the first time how all of this was weighing him down as well. He was just trying to look strong for his mom. This was a lot of the reasoning behind not wanting to tell them every little detail. Any little bit was already too much.

He pulled his keys out of his pocket. "Come on. There's a place in town we can grab a bite to eat."

Neither parent looked thrilled with the suggestion but Dean sincerely doubted it was for the same reasons.

Chapter Fourteen

Jamie sat on the picnic table bench at the rear of the vet clinic, watching a German shepherd puppy sniff around in the snow lumps while Cade walked a Border Collie named Sophie, a regular guest.

"Do you think Chris would take it wrong if I asked for a dog?"

Cade's attention turned to him. "Why haven't you asked him?"

"Because of..." He gave Cade a raised brow. "I didn't want to insult him, either."

"You could never do that," Cade said.

"Oh, I'm sure if I tried I could." He grinned, full of playful mischief. "But no, I don't *want* to. I've just always wanted a dog. None of the animals here seem to be affected by you guys when you're around," he offered, sounding a bit hopeful.

"We don't have an affect on other animals like this, not the way you're probably thinking. Could you see us all being vets if that happened?" He moved closer and sat beside him, letting Sophie and the pup nose at each other. "The wolf is another story."

"I know Bear and Biscuit aren't scared of him."

"They're used to him. A wild wolf? Don't count on it."

Jamie nodded, keeping one hand in his coat pocket. He bit on his lips, probably warming them in the cold. "So, should I?"

"Do you want one?"

Jamie tilted his head, watching the puppy paw and then bump against Sophie. "The house gets so quiet when he's here and I'm at home. I was also thinking about talking to Duncan, maybe doing something with SAR here."

"Do you think he's going to be around for it?"

Jamie gave him a knowing smile.

Cade laughed. "I swear, I'm going to start calling you yenta, or something."

Jamie burst out with laughter, a billowing cloud appearing on the air. "What, because I'm right about them? Because I told Chris after meeting Dean the first time that we'd be seeing more of him?"

"Don't look so smug." Cade pushed on Jamie's shoulder.

"I think it's worth the effort, that's all. Search and rescue," he quickly pointed out. "Not finding all of you your mates. Not taking that up as a second calling."

Cade huffed, but smiled. "You are, and shall always be, a brat."

"Thank you!" He tipped an imaginary cap.

This was one of the many reasons Cade liked having Jamie not only as a brother-in-law, but as a friend. Jamie wasn't afraid of any of them, of asking for advice, of talking, of anything, really. He was a genuine kind of guy.

"If you think it's something you can devote yourself to, then ask him. I can tell you this, he'll expect you to adopt or rescue."

Jamie gave him a stern look. "Like I'd buy a dog. With working here, treating them—"

Cade quickly raised a hand, cutting him off. He hadn't meant to rile him. "Could be another way Duncan could help you find the right nose."

Jamie scowled at him, but faced forward after. "True. I do like working here, but I want to do more." He scratched at a doggy head and floppy ears. "I've also been thinking about those cocking classes I talked about over Christmas. I'm going to do a summer program. I don't want to be the next big name, but I enjoy feeding people."

"You realize you'll never get rid of us," Cade joked. Jamie had received so many compliments on his ham, Chris will have to fight off guests for next year's party.

Jamie's face lit with pleasure. "I'm good with that."

The back door of the clinic opened and a bundled up Quade sauntered out. "You two ready to call it done?"

They stood and guided their charges inside. A quick rub down with a towel, fresh food and water, and they were done for the night.

Cade smiled when he neared his home and spotted Dean's car at the curb again. The other man stood from the car when he turned into the drive.

"Where are your parents?"

"At their hotel, at least for now."

Cade nudged his head toward the house, a signal to follow. He doubted Dean would disagree.

Once inside, they hung up their coats.

"Honestly, I'm trying to convince them to go home."

"Not working?"

He groaned audibly and plopped down onto one of Cade's living room chairs. He put his hands into his face. "Mom is shredded. I hate reminding her of Daniel's dying."

"You're not responsible for his death, or for her tenacity."

Dean sagged into the chair, gazing at Cade with some of the saddest eyes. "No, but I'm not leaving. I have my life here. Friends." He stood after staring deeply for several seconds at him to clear the gap between them. "You."

Cade simply wrapped him up and held on. "You've been reliving that night, haven't you?"

Dean nodded. "I— There was nothing I could do. I was inside. He was outside. The shot was point blank. And now…" A shuddering breath rocked him against Cade's chest. The heat blasted against his neck when he released it. "They never blamed me."

"But you do," he said quietly. Dean didn't deny it.

"Now that the bar is gone, she is determined to get me home."

Cade threaded a hand through Dean's hair. "But this is your home," he said, hiding the twinge of panic. If Dean left, Cade would follow. There was no other option for him. It was a future he didn't want to think about, though. Too many decisions he didn't want to have to face if it came down to it.

"Have you eaten?" Cade asked, changing the subject.

"A late lunch with them."

"I have something to make here, if you want."

"Okay."

Dean disentangled himself from Cade, and he reluctantly let him go. Staring at the man he'd held, he knew if he chose to go north, Cade would follow. He had no idea about packs, jobs, or how he'd deal with being away from his brothers, but if Dean needed his parents, Cade wouldn't hold him back. He didn't know when it happened, when Dean had taken priority, even over his own family, but he had. It wouldn't matter how difficult it would be, it would have to be done.

After changing clothes, Cade rummaged in the kitchen to make dinner.

While he was doing that, Dean's cell phone rang. "Hey, Jamie." Cade caught his gaze and Dean smiled from where he leaned on a shoulder out of Cade's way. "Yeah, they're here for a couple more days probably. Why? Oh. I'm sure they'd love it. What time? Bring the... I am not saying that!" Dean burst out with laughter. "He's standing right here! Yeah, yeah. Okay. See you tomorrow night. Thanks." He disconnected the call, swallowing more of his laughter.

He tipped the phone in Cade's direction, saying, "Your brother-in-law is a menace," then slid it into a pocket.

Cade shook his head in answer. "Repeat after me, *brraaat*."

Dean chuckled.

"What's the plan?"

"Dinner at their place, tomorrow night. He said about six thirty."

Cade nodded. "Not surprised." He knew having family, being part of a family that cared and supported each other, was very important to Jamie.

"Let me call them so they don't make other plans." He turned away for the living room to make the call.

Once they were seated to eat, Cade asked, "Did you find out anything else after going to the station?"

"No, not yet. I tried to call the detective on the way here, but he didn't answer. I wanted to know who this guy is and why he's connected to Daniel's shooting." Dean grimaced. "What did I ever do to him? It was my brother who died."

Cade reached and encircled Dean's forearm.

Dean leaned over his plate, confusion marring his features. "I just don't get it. The fire, the roof, this…" He motioned to his neck. "Daniel's murderer is in jail. He's not even up for parole for another fifteen years."

Cade wondered the same. It could be anyone, and the knowledge that it was possibly someone tied to Daniel was eating at Dean. "When did it happen?"

"Six years ago. I don't think I ever said. I'm thirty-four." A hint of a sheepish grin appeared.

Cade snickered lowly. "I guessed you were older than me." That didn't matter to him. "So, if it's connected to Daniel, but his killer isn't a possibility, who?"

Dean frowned. "Family? A friend wanting revenge? And why now?" He used his fork to stab at food, pushing it around. "I honestly have no fucking clue." Absently, he rubbed at his neck. Cade didn't doubt he'd be forgetting that anytime soon.

"What are you doing next?" Cade asked a few minutes later.

Dean glanced up from a nearly empty plate. "The insurance has finally closed the claim. They're issuing funds next week. I just need to decide what to do with them. Buy, or build, and where."

"Where?" Cade echoed softly. "Would you be willing to bring it to Silo? Or at least closer?"

Dean shrugged. "I would need to apply for serving licenses with the city. That wouldn't be an issue. But... It's a heck of a nightly drive to Cassan," he said with a leading hint in his tone.

"Who said anything about you staying in Cassan?" Cade retorted with mock severity. They slowly grinned in mutual understanding.

"So I guess that's your way of saying I'm moving in?"

"Unless you don't want to," he said, sitting away a fraction, hoping he wasn't pushing too hard. They'd come a long way since Christmas, but he didn't want to give Dean more to stress over.

Dean reached and curled a hand behind Cade's neck, stopping his retreat, tugging him close. His lips touched Cade's. "I'm kinda happy with the guy I'm dating right now. Let me think about it. Closer does sounds like a good idea."

"Just kind of happy, huh?"

Dean nipped at his upper lip, giving Cade a jolt to his spinal nerves. "We're good," he said.

Relief flooded Cade. Maybe someday he'd even be mother approved.

* * * *

Cade opened Jamie's front door the next evening. He smiled when he snagged on Dean's gaze. The return gaze was a little drawn, weary. Cade tilted his head in question, but Dean just shook his head.

He opened the door. "Come on in," he invited. Dean's parents trailed him. "Let me put up your coats."

They all gave them to Cade and he carried them to the bedroom, putting them with everyone else's. Cade turned to discover Dean slipping into the bedroom and quietly shutting the door.

Cade didn't hesitate. He opened his arms and Dean met him halfway.

"Bad day?"

"One word: Mom." Dean nuzzled into his throat.

A tense Dean almost melted into Cade, relaxing against his frame. "What does your dad say?"

"He thinks I should go back with them, but he's at least willing to let me make the decision. Mom…" He groaned, burrowing harder against Cade. "She's all or nothing, and the alternative isn't an option."

"So she's not going to relent?"

"I really don't think so."

"Where does that put you?"

Dean grumbled. "Honestly, at odds with her, because I'm not leaving."

Cade held on a little tighter. "How about if you promise to see them in a few months? When did you last visit?"

"About three years ago."

Cade's thoughts circled. "So if you make plans to see them more often, would that help?"

"If it will get her to let up, I'd promise almost anything," he grumped, though jokingly. "Just can't promise to move." He kissed Cade's neck and straightened. "Better get back out there. Come over tonight?" As worn as he looked, Cade knew he couldn't say no.

Cade nodded and after a final quick kiss, reluctantly released him.

"There they are," Maya teased, the first to spot them. "Did you boys get your hello kiss out of the way?"

"Quade," Cade said with as much suffering as he could pour into his voice. "She's not wearing her muzzle again."

Maya laughed. "Ah, you know you love me."

"No, he loves you." He motioned to his brother. "I think you're a pain in the rump."

"I thought I had that privileged spot," Jamie piped up from the kitchen.

"Can't win, can you?" Dean asked. Amusement was making his eyes glitter now. Cade knew Dean was already accustomed to their familial bickering. He was just glad to see the strain he'd carried walking in the door had faded.

Chris handed them both filled glasses. "Try this."

"Is it loaded?" Cade asked. He'd willingly try it if it were.

"No. Just drink it. It's tea."

Cade took a sip and Dean copied him. "Wow." He licked his lips and took another big drink. He spotted Jamie watching them expectantly. With Cade's approval, he smiled huge.

"See? I told you," Chris said to Jamie. "I wasn't being biased."

"Yes, you were, and I expect you to be," Jamie informed him. He carried two more to Dean's parents, offering them with smiles. "Thanks for coming."

"Thanks for inviting us," Ann replied, accepting the glass. "Is it sweet?"

"With fruit juice, and only a little. No added sugar."

She seemed surprised, but nodded, taking a small sip. That led to a much larger one, which had Jamie smiling broader. After making sure they were comfortable, he returned to the kitchen. Cade was grateful to see Maya talking to Ann, while Chris and Quade were talking with Trent. Jamie was working on something in the kitchen.

"I'm going to see if he needs any help," Cade said.

"Okay." Dean squeezed his hand before he walked away.

"Need any help?" Cade asked, wondering how he could. The table looked nice. It was already set, and Jamie had decorated with a hollowed log with small candles for a centerpiece. He had no idea where he got it, but it looked good.

"Thanks," Jamie replied, adding butter to a dish. "It's almost ready." Jamie surreptitiously gazed at Dean's parents, then said, "They're nice people."

Cade did the same. "They seem to be," he offered.

"Oh?"

"Nothing," he muttered. He wasn't about to say it. He knew Ann didn't think he was good enough, but geez. When was the last time he'd had *that* problem? He really didn't know why Ann was so against him. If she thought disapproval would pressure Dean to return with them, he honestly didn't know.

Jamie patted his arm. "Don't worry about it. They're having a good time." He turned and put the bowl on the table. "Soup's on!"

"It smells wonderful," Maya said when she stopped at a chair.

"Thank you." They all sat. "I actually owe Dean."

"You do?" he asked, surprised as he paused in loading his plate.

"Chris knows I want to cook better, but it was your suggestion to check out the internet courses. I did."

"And?" Quade asked.

"I'm going to enroll for the summer semester at the community college in Stiller Springs. I'll also see if there's anything else that I can take in the same window, maybe something vet tech related. Might as well make it work for me."

Chris had reached over and covered one of Jamie's hands as he'd spoken.

"That sounds great," Dean said.

Everyone dug in and ate, complimenting Jamie between bites.

"How long have you been together?" Ann asked Jamie a few minutes later.

"Only since the spring," Jamie explained. "Dad kicked me out and Chris found me about a week later."

"Why would he do that?" Ann exclaimed.

"Because I told him I was gay. There was a guy I wanted to ask out back where I grew up, but I couldn't because Dad would want to know who he was, why he was around. So I told him. He assaulted me." He smiled at Chris. "It was a good thing I was found, too."

"I will never understand parents, anyone, who can treat another like that," Trent grumbled. "Being gay is no more a decision than what color your hair is when you're born."

"The only problem with being gay is no grandchildren." Ann sighed despondently. "I really was hoping for them."

"Mom." Dean rubbed into his eyes with stiff fingers. "Don't do this. Not right now."

"It's okay," Cade offered, noticing how everyone else had mostly stopped eating, giving Dean all their attention. He doubted that was helping at all. He slid a hand under the table and rested it in comfort on Dean's thigh. "We've already talked about that."

Ann faced him, surprise pitching her voice a little when she asked, "You have?"

"It was more a case of I explained what I hope for, and to see if he was agreeable, but, yes. So that makes it 'not a problem'."

"But... How?"

"Surrogacy or adoption. I lean toward adoption because someone out there, hundreds of thousands really, already need a loving home." He faced Dean and caught the softest gleam of understanding in his gaze. "There are things we need to talk about, but we can't. Not yet."

"Why not?" Ann asked. He almost replied, but Dean cut him off.

"Because you want me to come home so bad," Dean remarked testily. He twisted on the seat to face his parents. "If I come home to make you happy, I lose Cade. I lose this family. I lose everything I've spent the last eight years building."

"But the bar is gone," Ann pointed out. "You can do the same at home."

"Yes and no. It can be rebuilt, and I can start over, anywhere. That much is true. But there's more here than just the bar." He turned enough to catch first Cade's gaze then those around the table. "I like being here. I love this crazy family."

Cade's heart tripped hearing that.

Facing his mother, he scowled in clear displeasure. "And I'm very tired of deflecting your conniving to change it. I don't appreciate you bringing it up here, tonight, either." He withdrew from the table. "I'm sorry. Excuse me?" He spun and vanished down the hallway. Cade knew he was probably going to hide in the spare for a few minutes.

Ann put a hand to her face, then covered her mouth. "I'm sorry," she finally gasped. Trent put an arm around her until she calmed.

Cade released a slow breath. He wanted to follow so badly, but he waited a few seconds. "Please understand Ann."

"I'm trying. I know I haven't done that well enough." She smiled shakily at her husband and sat easier on her chair. An air full of apology settled around her. "I haven't been fair to you, either. You have a wonderful family. I'm sorry, to all of you. He's right. I just want him to be happy."

"Then give me the chance to do that. Give him the chance to make up his own mind," Cade said.

When she didn't continue, Cade guessed it was up to him to make everything right again. He excused himself and went hunting for his man.

Chapter Fifteen

When the door opened, Dean knew it was Cade without looking. He found him in the spare, sitting on the bed, staring off into space.

"I'm sorry. That was so rude."

Cade sat at his side, ignoring the pile of winter coats. "It's okay. I think she's ready to listen now, though."

"Yeah?" Dean doubted it. Fighting with his mother was exhausting.

"Yeah. I think seeing why you want to stay aside from the bar's history matters."

Dean rested with his temple to Cade's shoulder. A single arm snaked around his back and held him steady. "She's never had a problem with me being gay, so that isn't it. It's because I want to stay here. My life is here. The life I have is fine with me. I don't want to change it. Is this really that much to ask for her to understand?"

"I don't think so, but I'm part of the equation. As Jamie accused Chris, I'm very biased."

Dean snickered. "Those two." He tilted and gazed at Cade's profile. There were so many reasons he wasn't going to bend to his mother's wants. It was no surprise that the biggest reason was holding on to him. He honestly cared for Cade. Through misunderstandings and the troubles he'd faced, through the shocks Cade had given him, Cade was steady, and still stood by him. Dean wasn't done with finding out how far they could go, and if he were being honest, he hoped they never did find out where the finish line was. The idea of having a family, of having Cade there when he came home was one in a million. He wanted that. He wanted Cade, which meant his unusual family, his secrets, and everything that came with him.

Cade snuggled him closer. "She did say she wants you to be happy."

He scoffed. "When?"

"Just now. I think she means it."

Dean didn't reply. He'd wait and see. He knew his mother. She was probably only regrouping for the next round of arguments.

"Come on. My brothers are going to start taking bets if we don't get out there."

Dean reached and cupped Cade's jaw, bringing him close before he could pull away. A quiet groan filled the gap between them right before their lips touched. The kiss was heady, sweet, and filled with longing for more. "Still coming tonight?" Dean asked when they parted.

"I'll be right behind you."

They lingered over the soft kisses for a few more minutes. Dean couldn't help it. He *did* like the man's kisses.

"Besides," Cade said as they stood to leave the bedroom. "You're stuck with me now. Even if you decide it's for the best to leave, I'll be right there with you."

Dean looked over his shoulder. "What does that mean?"

"Wolves mate as pairs, for life. It translates to us and our mates as fidelity on steroids."

Dean's hand stopped on the knob. "So…" He frowned. Mating? For life? This was the first he'd heard of this little concept. *Definitely not so little.* "What does that mean?"

"I've already bonded with you. I go where you go."

"Wait." Dean turned and put his spine to the door. His brain did a quick rerun of the last few weeks. *Nope. No recollection.* "Don't I get a say in this?" He wanted Cade, but wasn't this a little…*fast*? Christ, he cared, but there was no guarantee they'd make it to Easter. He knew what he wanted to see happen. He also knew what the odds were on any relationship. There were emotions, family, kids, houses… Any number of decisions to work through, but just like that, he's supposed to accept this decision was already made and he just had to fall in line? Definitely something he would remember.

And he didn't.

Cade frowned. "I thought…you did."

"No. I would have remembered this conversation," he said, consternation growing. "I understood that things would be different with you. I *didn't* know it was already decided. What if you find out there's something about me you can't stand?"

Cade relaxed, offering a small smile. "Already cleared that hurdle. I wasn't expecting my mate to be a man."

Dean threw up a hand and blocked Cade. "So all that bullshit before… You're still not able to say you're gay?" And he's *now* saying he *hates the fact* that Dean's a guy? Not the warm and fuzzy kind of revelation going on here.

"I'm not gay." Cade scowled. "I have no interest in men. Only in you."

"Fucker," Dean cursed. "That's *bullshit*. So what? Are you going to start sniffing after some big tit blonde next?"

"Sniffing." Cade had the audacity to snicker.

Dean's jaw clenched as he fought snarls of anger. He wasn't playing around. Cade must have noticed because he sliced off the laughter quickly.

"No. I haven't looked at a woman in more than two years. I was attracted to you from the beginning. Almost from the first minute we met, and when I got to know you, it became impossible to fight that and the wolf's need to be with you."

Dean shoved. Hard. Cade stumbled back a step. "I get it. You're not gay. You don't really care who or what you end up with, is that it? But your wolf said *Hey, he looks good*, so I was it, huh? And it doesn't matter if you actually like me, or care, or fuck, can you even love a man?"

"I don't know."

That stopped Dean cold. That wasn't what he wanted to hear.

Dean didn't know what he'd expected, but it hadn't been this. "This is total bullshit," he hissed.

"What has you so mad?"

"You can't fucking figure it out?" he snapped.

"I've been honest. I've told you everything."

"You never *once* said anything about there being no choice in this, about being your mate regardless of whether or not it was something I was ready for, or wanted," he finished. He opened the door. "I'm taking my parents back to their hotel. Do not follow me."

"Dean," he said. He raised a hand to catch the door.

"No. You don't get it. I want to see where this goes, but you forgot to mention that little detail."

Cade's brow furrowed.

"I'm not getting into a relationship with anyone who is with me out of duty because some crazy, whacked out spirit says you have no choice in this. If you're not gay, if you don't *even like* men, then just what the hell are you doing? Because let me say this: I *do* have a choice."

"I'm not gay. I never have been."

"Do you hear yourself? So what? I'm supposed to accept that after a lifetime of women, you've suddenly decided that I'm it? One man in the entire world?"

"Not decided. It's just the way it is."

Dean rolled his eyes. "I give up." He tugged the door, ignoring Cade's reticence to letting him out. He wasn't going to battle pigheaded all night. "I'll call in a few days. Maybe."

"Don't do this. Please."

The aching panic in Cade's voice almost made him rethink the last ten minutes.

Almost. He fished jackets off the bed and stormed out of the room. He interrupted the discussion and laughter at the table. "Mom, Dad. I'm sorry. We need to go."

"Is everything all right?" Ann asked, concerned. She rose from her seat though.

"Dean," Cade pleaded quietly from behind him.

"No. I'm sorry. Thank you Chris, Jamie. I'll make it up to you both."

Jamie stood also. "I understand."

"Honestly, you very well might," he replied. "I'll call you." Jamie nodded, clearly avoiding looking at Cade. Dean helped his mother put on her coat. "Good night, Quade. Maya. Thanks again."

"Ann, be sure to let us know when you get home, okay?" Maya piped up, standing to say her goodbyes as well.

"Thank you all. You've been very kind." She hugged Maya and smiled. Trent shook Chris' hand.

Dean herded his parents out the front door and to the car. "I'm very sorry," he said, getting behind the wheel.

"Did you two fight?" his mother asked.

"Yes, and I don't want to talk about it."

Ann merely nodded. "Okay."

Dean slid her a quick look. That was way too easy. Instead of waiting for her to start poking, he put the car in reverse and turned around for the driveway. The drive home was the longest hour in his life.

* * * *

"What did you do?" Jamie asked.

Not accusing, which Cade was grateful for. He could feel his world unraveling and it killed him. Cade plopped onto his seat. He braced his head on open palms over cold food, ignoring it completely. He'd lost his appetite. Possibly forever.

"I fucked up. I just don't really know what I did."

Silence thickened, then, "Maya, could you help me clean up?"

She gathered plates. "Sure." She kissed Quade on the cheek and trailed after Jamie with her hands full. The sound of water and dishes being rinsed provided the sense of a wall between them. At least it wasn't going to be four against one.

"Okay, what did you say?" Quade braced his elbows on the table.

"I told him if it came down to it and he had to leave for his parents, I'd be there with him. I understand I can't keep him from his family." Cade rubbed the heels of his hands into his eye sockets. Somehow in the last ten minutes, everything had fallen apart. He was trying to be understanding, supportive, and all he'd managed to do was piss off Dean.

"That can't be all of it. Maya and I discussed the exact same thing. It came down to her or the pack. She gave me the pack."

Cade raised bleary eyes to study his brother. "And I offered the same thing. I said here or his family." How was that so wrong?

"You're missing a step, or not giving us the whole story," Chris said.

"What step?"

"What caused the fight to begin with?"

Cade sighed. He pushed his plate out of the way with an elbow. "I told him I'd go with him because I'd already bonded with him. That there wasn't any reason to discuss it."

Chris and Quade shared a startled look.

"Oh, shit," Quade whispered. "You didn't?"

"Didn't what?" Cade was beginning to feel exhausted with the whole discussion. He was dying to go after Dean, but knew he wouldn't be welcome. This time, he knew Dean wouldn't open the door.

"Without him knowing?" Quade narrowed his eyes. "Damn it, Cade. You married him by pack law without him even knowing it."

"What?" Cade sat up, chills hitting his shoulders. "What are you talking about?"

"The bond," Chris answered. He crossed his arms on the table and leaned over them. "Don't you remember Dad's warnings?"

"No." Cade blinked. He really didn't.

"He may not realize what you've done, but he obviously understands the underlying definition of what it means to be bonded or he wouldn't be so furious."

"I don't need pack permission to bond. Do I?" he asked fearfully as an afterthought. He waited with dread until one of them answered.

"No," Chris replied.

Cade sagged with relief. "Then what's the problem?"

Quade tipped his head in aggravated disbelief, saying, "Dean gets you drunk and manages to get you to say I do, without you knowing. Eight hours later you wake up and Bam! You're married."

Cade shook his head. "But I ca—" His eyes widened as the truth hit him square between the eyes. "Fuck! No! No, no. I swear. It's not what I wanted to do to him."

"Tell him that," Chris advised. "Because that is exactly what you did."

Now what Dean had said made sense and it made his stomach roll with self-loathing. There had been no choice, no warning, and definitely no discussion of it at all. "I didn't mean to do that to him. It was... It just happened!" He planted his face into uplifted palms and shuddered. He had no idea it would work against Dean, not just *for* Cade. "I thought it would all work itself out. He's the one the wolf chose. How could it be wrong?"

"The wolf? Don't you want him?" Chris asked, tension subduing his voice in concern.

Cade lurched upright. "What's that mean?"

Chris studied him. "Are you gay? Are you bi? How do you feel about Dean being male?"

Cade swallowed thickly. "I'm not gay. I know that." Cade didn't understand what the difference was. He wanted to be with Dean. He cared for him. The wolf wanted him. Why did he have to say he was gay? Why did it matter?

Chris didn't comment, only scowling in deepening disappointment. Quade wasn't as lenient. "What do you mean by that?"

"What difference does it make?" Cade snapped, growing irritated.

Quade pushed. "Because it means everything to Dean. If you're not gay, or at least willing to be open to loving a man, then you've pushed Dean into a corner."

Cade shoved away from the table. "I don't need this!"

"Sit. Down."

All three heads whipped to land gazes on Jamie. Fire sparked in his blue eyes.

"Sit your shithead ass down." He approached the table but didn't take his seat. "All three of you are shithead animals." Chris twitched. "Don't even think it."

"What did I do?" Chris gaped at him.

"I'll talk to you later," Jamie warned. He stood over Cade and pinned him to his seat with a steely glare. "Let me put this bluntly. Dean is human. He is not *pack*. He *is* gay. He is half in love with you whether he wants to admit it or not. You, you cretin, bonded him. A human. Let that sink in." Jamie scowled at all of them.

Chris reached for Jamie's hand. "Baby?"

"No, you and I are fine. We had a different tangent to get to this point." He squeezed once then released him. "Cade on the other hand." He sighed. "I can't tell you what Dean sees or what he's thinking, but I can take a damn good shot in the dark. He's dealing with seven kinds of shit right now, and you just told him that you'd go with him, anywhere, because you're bonded. Oh, gee. Thanks." Jamie scoffed, rolling his eyes in sheer exasperation. "And then you have the nerve to emphasize the fact that you're not *really* gay, but hey, he's what the wolf wants."

Cade slouched. "That's not—"

"Trust me, that's what he heard. That's exactly what you just told your brothers. I heard every word, and a few from the argument with Dean. If you're only with him because the wolf chose him then you've fucked up bad."

"Look, I've tried to figure this out."

Jamie leaned on his knuckles and got in Cade's face. "Try. Harder. Telling him to his face that you can't do more because you can't accept that it will make you gay, is bullshit. Whichever sexuality label you feel most comfortable with, doesn't matter. What does matter is that you're open to loving him as a man."

Cade felt heat on his cheeks as memories flashed before him.

"Oh, God!" Jamie cried, throwing up his hands. "Not for sex! Are you really that dense?"

"Sorry. It was the first thing to pop into my mind." He rolled a shoulder, biting the embarrassed smile off before it could grow. "It really wasn't intentional."

"No wonder he lost patience with you tonight." Jamie put a hand on Cade's shoulder. "Quit using the wolf as your scapegoat to being in a same-sex relationship. You are more than the wolf you carry."

"But...women...since I was fourteen," Cade choked, rife with confusion. "And now...this?" He thought he'd handled it, now it was looking like all he'd done was buried his head in the sand trying to make it go away.

Jamie lowered to a crouch, searching upward into Cade's eyes. "That's something only you can answer. It was the one thing only I could answer."

Cade looked across the table. Both Chris and Quade were silent. Cade's head ached as much as his heart and neither were giving him any answers.

"Was it something I did?" Quade asked cautiously.

"Of course not," Cade asserted.

"We always challenged each other," Quade said, not convinced.

"That's what brothers do," Chris said. "But no, it wasn't anything you did. Neither of you could influence me on that level. Quade, you did nothing to Cade."

Cade nodded, rubbing his temples. "But that's where… Geez. You *knew*." He raised his chin a fraction to find Chris across from him. "I thought…and now I don't know anymore."

Jamie enveloped him in a close hug. Cade leaned into that hold, lost.

"I think you do know," he said gently. "You can do this. It's you caring for him, not the wolf telling you it's what you have to do."

"I know." Cade really shouldn't be making it sound like the only reason he was with Dean was because the wolf had picked him. It sounded like he'd been chosen out of a police lineup! No wonder he'd been hurt and insulted. Hell, he'd have reacted worse and he knew it.

He sighed, maybe not any closer to accepting, but he knew he was getting closer to understanding all of this, himself especially. "So I guess saying sorry, again, is a good place to start?"

Jamie stroked his hair. "Sorry is usually a safe place, yes." He winked toward Chris. "We all have practice with that one."

"Is it safe?" Maya peeked around the rear hallway. "You're all alive. That's good."

Quade chuckled and held out a hand for her. "It's safe. Where'd you go?"

"I didn't think Cade would want to feel ganged up on, so I went to go share secrets with Bear." She scooted in to sit on Quade's lap. He scrubbed her hands between his larger ones to warm them up. She'd snuck out without her jacket, so Cade bet she was cold. He almost envied his brother in that moment, having that closeness.

Jamie gave a last squish of a squeeze and he joined Chris, leaning into his side rather than claiming his lap. Chris circled him with an arm at his hips, framing his waist, as close as they could get.

Now that most of Cade's crises were handled, or at least illuminated enough for him to deal with, Cade studied both couples as they began to relax and chat quietly. All of them were comfortable in their skin, in their pairings. It didn't matter the sex, because they were more than bonded. They were in love. Cade could see it.

It didn't matter.

He rubbed a hand down his face. "I have to go." Before he said what he was thinking out loud. He never wanted to have to say it. It was enough that he finally recognized what it was holding him back. Knowing it didn't make him like the truth anymore, either.

Sliding behind the steering wheel of the vet truck, he corrected himself. There was one person he owed the full truth to. There was one person who deserved to know what this revelation was, because it would affect the both of them, and everything they were meant to be.

Cade just hoped Dean would listen.

Chapter Sixteen

Dean unlocked his front door to get inside and went to hit the light switch. "Fuck!" In aggravation, he flipped it a few more times, but no, nothing changed. No lights. "Son of a bitch." He'd dropped off his parents at their hotel after a tense ride to Cassan. He knew his mother was itching to pry into the argument he'd had with Cade, but she'd somehow managed to not badger him. After all of that, he comes home to a dark house.

Walking inside, he wondered how long the power had been out. He aimed for the kitchen and opened the freezer. A cloud of cold popped out. Not long. *Good.* He started pawing through drawers looking for the flashlight. He knew he had one. He really hoped it had batteries that worked.

He used the screen light from his phone for a dim halo as he searched. He slammed the drawer shut. It wasn't there. Damn it, where did he put it last time?

The temperature was dropping without the heater kicking on. He could feel it against bare skin. He started digging in another drawer. Wind pushed against the house, making it creak and groan. Sounded like another front. Not a good night to have lost power.

Hunting in another drawer, his back was turned to the hallway to the second half of the house. It wasn't a very large home, a single-wide trailer. Three bedrooms with the kitchen and living room separating them, and one of those rooms was nothing but storage. He wasn't even close to being the first owner, but like he'd told Cade, how much did he really need? He'd shared a place with Daniel, but after his death, he'd needed something that wasn't a constant reminder when he had Gemini's for that.

Maybe the phone could give off enough light to at least check the breaker box. There had to be a reason it went out. The bill had been paid, so it had to be something electrical.

He glanced out the kitchen window to the front yard. It was dark, overcast, and the wind was picking up surface powder and tossing it around like a dust storm. There was something definitely moving in. The last good snowfall had been several days before, which meant they were due for the next wave.

He shivered. He did not want to be in a powerless house overnight. His phone started singing. He sent the call to voicemail, well aware by the tone who was calling. He wasn't ready to talk to Cade. Dean was still pissed at him, with plenty of reasons to stay that way.

His hand lowered.

The instantly biting pressure around his neck shocked him. He jerked for it with a clawed hand as it painfully started to slice through skin.

The stranglehold held him immobile, pinned between the body behind him and the counter before him.

Scratching at the thin wire around his neck was pointless as the pressure increased. His jaw ached as he clenched his teeth, jerking his body to unbalance the man behind him. They struggled, weaving and bouncing around the kitchen.

Dean hunted with a hand but couldn't get enough backward lean to find the man's head. Air was beginning to burn as he labored to breathe. His throat felt on fire. The line of pain was intense. Each jerk of limbs, of bodies, sawed the wire a little deeper into soft flesh.

He bent and spun, unable to shake the weight of the clinging man. The garrote was anchoring him to Dean.

Sparks popped in front of his eyes, scattering like wild comets.

The level of pain bursting from the pressing slice of the garrote had never been felt in his life. He refused to give in to it.

They crashed into the refrigerator, toppling things to the floor from above as they struggled. A few things shattered, or rolled. He didn't have the capacity place what they had been. He tried to trip his attacker, but there just wasn't a way to take him off balance. The man avoided elbows like a matador avoided horns. He pulled on arms, yanked on clothing; he had absolutely no leverage to disentangle the person behind him.

A knock on the door was followed by, "Dean, open up. I'm sorry."

Dean almost passed out as the pressure increased with deadly intent into his neck. No more drawing it out. The man behind him wanted to finish this. Like a twist tie was being wound behind his neck, the noose shrank, cutting deeper. He pushed with one last gathering of strength, knocking them both into the refrigerator again. It shuddered and shook. They rebounded into the wall, creating an explosive *thud*. He gasped as the pressure moved, increased, jumped.

Seared his flesh. He felt the slick slice as it dug deeper into skin. He was losing.

He was going to die.

"Dean!" Cade rattled the door impatiently.

His vision was going gray. The darkness surrounding him thickened. His chest raged with the strain.

The door exploded inward with a hard boot kick.

His legs went out from under him, unable to hold his weight any longer. His lungs screamed for air. His throat... Blood. It was soaking his front. Pain. Aching numbness.

An unholy growl was followed by a cry. The tension around his neck vanished. He collapsed face first to the floor, gasping, holding a hand to his throat. He shuddered in agony and then darkness enveloped him.

* * * *

Cade stopped behind Dean's car. The house was utterly dark. He had to be home. Cade didn't think he had that much of a head start on him that he'd already be in bed, but maybe he was.

It felt eerie, though. There was absolutely *no* light, from anywhere around the house. Cade frowned. A sense of disquiet pervaded the air. Wind blew, but the rest...felt...*off.*

He climbed the steps and knocked on the door. "Dean. Open up. I'm sorry."

He waited, listening, hoping Dean would give him one more chance. Expecting a light to pop on, he stood on the step. A loud thud caught his attention, locking his muscles in anticipation. The impact rocked the whole trailer. "Dean!" He tried the knob, cursing that it was locked.

"Forgive me if I'm wrong," he whispered. He kicked in the door.

Pitch black filled the house to every corner, with only the slightest tinge of illumination through the windows. Harsh panting and scuffled feet whipped his head in the direction of the kitchen.

He barely acknowledged the growl when it filled his throat. A running start. His entire body launching through the air. The *crash* they made as he took the man to the ground. It was disjointed and done completely instinctively. Cade held him down with a relentless grip and punched him. Just once. He went limp instantly.

"Dean!" He shook the man he straddled then lurched away. "Dean! Talk to me!"

Scrambling over the person's body, he reached Dean's side, ignoring the oddities on the floor. Blood ran from the wound around his neck. "Dean!" He hunted for a pulse and almost sobbed when he found it.

"I got you," he whispered. With care, Cade rolled him to his side, jerking off his coat to rest his head on then tried to see what he could find to staunch the blood coming from his wounded neck. He dug kitchen towels out of the drawer and used them to pack against Dean's throat. "Stay with me, babe. Please." The bleeding was lessening. That was a good sign. He hadn't reached a vein or artery.

Withdrawing his phone, he called for emergency. His own panting was slowly evening out from sheer panic.

Cade kept a finger to Dean's pulse and a hawk's watch on his breathing. So many things could happen. Blood into his lungs, a collapsed passage… He tried hard to not let those thoughts distract his vigilance over him.

Lights and sirens eventually lit up the frozen world outside the gaping doorway.

"In here!" Cade shouted. He hadn't moved from Dean's side, and wasn't about to. Not until they were ready to put him on the stretcher for the trip to the hospital. "I'll be right behind you, babe." He kissed Dean's forehead and let the EMTs take him away.

The wire had done a lot of damage. His anger boiled up again when he saw it as the EMTs started to treat him beneath better lights with a wrap to slow blood.

"Why is it so dark?" Officer Archer was playing with the light switch. They'd dragged out Dean's assailant in cuffs, still groggy and incoherent.

"I don't know. It was like this when I got here." He gathered his coat, kicking the kitchen towels to the side to be picked up and tossed later. "I'm following that ambulance. You deal with whoever you have in handcuffs."

"Will you be with him?"

"For the rest of my life," Cade said, waiting to be challenged.

Kelly grunted. "I'll be in touch in the morning to see if he's awake. I'll have questions for both of you by then."

"By then, I might have answers," Cade replied. He checked for his phone, spotting Dean's on the floor. He grabbed it and dropped it into a pocket. "Close the door on your way out." He had absolutely zilch desire to stay behind to help where he could do less than nothing. At least with Dean he could keep him company, and keep his own heart from shriveling in agonizing fear.

He jogged from the house for his truck. He didn't care what the police did. The only person that mattered was being carried away by the ambulance ahead of him.

He made phone calls on the drive. First to his brothers, then to Dean's parents. He told them he didn't know anything about his condition, only that the man behind the attacks was behind bars now.

"I'll keep in contact and let you know as I find out things," he said.

His mother, weeping, said thank you and hung up. He tossed the phone with his into the cup holder. It was all the information he had at the moment.

Dean was on his way to the hospital and the man behind it was going to jail. He didn't remember one second of the drive, just that he never once lost the spin of those strobing lights.

* * * *

Cade jerked awake when the door opened to Dean's room. He scrubbed his face, feeling grungy and twice as weary.

"How is he?" Jamie inched closer

"He's still out. They finished surgery about midnight. They said he wouldn't be awake until sometime in the morning."

Jamie handed over a large coffee. "Thought this might be better than the hospital brew."

"I'm positive it is," he replied, accepting it gratefully. He drew a sip, letting the still warm liquid coat his insides.

"What happened?"

"I don't really know." Cade pulled out his cell phone. It was a little after seven. Sleeping in a cramped and uncomfortable chair most of the night was not being appreciated by any part of Cade's body at the moment. He stretched gingerly, working out kinks, slowly drinking the coffee to wake up.

"Do you think this guy is behind everything?"

"I do. It was someone who knew Dean well enough to know when he'd be home, when he'd be at the bar." He rubbed the back of his neck, stretched his spine. He didn't think his shoulders were supposed to pop, but they did.

"Will he have permanent damage?"

"The doctors didn't say, but I don't think so."

Jamie nodded with the news. Then, "Chris gave you the next month off."

Cade straightened on the chair. "He didn't—"

Jamie gave him one of those unsettling looks that all of them had already learned meant business. "Take it, Cade. Dean needs you and you need the time with him. They can take care of the clinic between them."

He slumped in the chair, unwilling and too exhausted to fight. "Chris is lucky to have you."

Jamie rolled a shoulder, a slight smile fleetingly appearing then vanishing. "I'm the lucky one. Always will be." He patted Cade's shoulder. "I have to get back to Silo. Call when you find out anything."

Cade reached for the hand on his shoulder. "I will." He squeezed.

Jamie left and the room fell quiet again. Cade finished the coffee and dozed off and on, staying quiet and unobtrusive during nurse visits. So long as he didn't cause anyone issue, they'd left him alone. He behaved because he wasn't about to be thrown out.

Dean roused out of his drug-induced sleep about nine thirty.

Cade moved his chair closer as they waited for the staff nurse to come in and do a checkup. He held Dean's hand, keeping him from poking too curiously at the brace around his neck. It looked like he was wearing a white, cloth sausage.

Dean's lips moved, but the sound was very graveled and nearly inaudible.

"I know, babe. Don't talk."

Dean sighed, heavily shadowed eyes closing.

One of the head shift nurses came into the room. "Morning, Mr. Eckler," she greeted gently. She helped him adjust the bed so he could sit more upright then began taking a round of vitals to input on a computer she'd dragged in with her. "Okay," she said once that was done. "I need to ask you some questions. Don't try to talk. Can you lift your hand?"

Dean raised his free hand and gave a thumbs up.

"Good. I want you to answer these as truthfully as you can. If it's one to five, thumb down and then fingers." She showed him. "If it's six through ten, thumbs up and fingers, okay?"

Dean nodded.

"Good. How much pain does it cause you to breathe?"

Dean took slow breaths. Thumb down and three fingers.

"Good. I was hoping you'd say something along those lines. It's just sore from the trauma. Your esophageal passage wasn't injured."

"That's good, right?" Cade asked.

"Very good." She typed and asked some more questions about pain and where.

When she was almost done, Dean tapped Cade and pointed at his mouth.

"Water?" he asked.

Dean nodded.

The nurse answered for him. "I'll get you some ice chips for now. Your throat is fine, but you had damage to several tendons around your vocal chords. Excessive muscle movement over the next several days is going to be very uncomfortable."

"I'm guessing that's your way of saying it's going to hurt like hell if he pushes?"

She smirked. "Your words, but yes."

Dean's chest rose and fell as he breathed steadily. He nodded in understanding and made the *okay* finger sign.

When the nurse left, Dean tapped him again and motioned like he was writing.

"Sure. Let me see if I can find something. Rest until the ice gets here."

Cade left him relaxed on the bed, going to the nurses' station for a pen and pad. Saying thank you, he returned to find an orderly just dropping off the ice.

"Little sips," Cade warned.

Dean rolled his eyes but nodded.

Putting his finds on the table beside the bed, Cade helped slip chips of ice between Dean's lips.

It wasn't supposed to be anything beyond helping him, making sure he didn't overdo it right after having surgery.

What it turned into was an erotic tease.

The cool touch of the ice to Dean's lips, the soft capture of those same lips as he tongued the bits into his mouth off the spoon. The flick of lashes as sensation and relief collided on his features.

The moist sparkle of damp the ice left behind on his lips killed Cade with the desire to lick them.

Cade handed him the cup, clearing his throat. "Maybe… Maybe you should do it." He had swollen beyond uncomfortable in his jeans in the last ten minutes watching Dean make oral love to the spoon.

Dean huffed silently with humor but didn't refuse the cup. He took his time and Cade let him, not interrupting him.

When he was done, he set the emptied cup and spoon on the table next to him. He tapped the top of Cade's hand and motioned for the pad.

He wrote out a few things and handed it back.

Cade read them and started to answer each one.

"Yes, your parents know. I promised I'd call as soon as I learned something. No, I haven't talked to the police. They want to talk to both of us. I'm sure we'll be seeing them soon."

He lowered the pad to study Dean. "What happened?"

Dean reached for the pad and started writing. Cade gave him time as the words flowed from pen to paper.

When he read it, he trembled. *Jeee-sus.* So close. *So. Fucking. Close.* "Who is this guy?"

Dean shrugged.

"You don't have any ideas?"

No. A very small head shake.

"Maybe the police know."

He reached for the pad and wrote, *I hope so.* Then, *When do I go home?*

"I guess after the doctor looks in on you. Now that you're awake, I don't think you'll be here much longer."

He wrote out one more thing: *Thank you.*

Cade swallowed the rush of emotions that dared to clog his throat. "Always, babe. I'll always be there for you."

The use of babe caught Dean by surprise, his expressive eyes widening.

Cade cupped his hand. "We need to talk, but right now, all any of us want is to get you home."

Dean squeezed Cade's hand in undeniable agreement.

"Home," he breathed, a very raw whisper. *You.* He pointed to Cade, then to himself. *Me.*

"Yes. Home." Cade sighed in relief, pressing Dean's held hand to his cheek. Even after a million and one fuckups with Dean, his lover was giving him one more chance.

He promised he wouldn't waste this one.

Chapter Seventeen

Dean didn't argue when the trip home ended at Cade's place. Dean definitely wasn't going all the way to Cassan, according to Cade. He had called Kelly and told him to meet them both there that afternoon instead of making the drive to the hospital in the next county. Dean was sure Kelly had plenty of questions about last night.

"I'm going to put your things in the bedroom then start the tea water."

Dean just nodded. He was still feeling a little shaky. His body was out of sync with his brain. He sank down into the recliner and pushed backward to raise the footrest. Dean's cell phone rang not too long after Cade reappeared. Dean listened as Cade answered it, able to hear him talking to Ann.

"We're at my place now." Cade slid him a questioning look and Dean nodded. "Let me give you directions."

Dean zoned out to the rest of the conversation. He couldn't avoid his parents indefinitely. At least they were flying home soon. Dean was grateful Cade fielded phone calls because not long after his mother called, the detective was next. He agreed to come with the sheriff so Dean could answer everything with them both there.

A tap on his shoulder had him blearily blinking. He hadn't realized he'd zoned out and dozed off. A steaming mug waited for him. "It's pretty warm, so slow, okay?"

"Yes, Mother," Dean mouthed.

Cade chuckled.

Dean took a cautious sip. He had no idea how he was going to take the horse pills the hospital had prescribed, since even the smallest swallow tugged and ached at various points along his throat. The warmth felt good, though.

He wore a neck brace around his throat with gauze wrapped beneath to protect he'd forgotten how many stitches. The brace kept him from straining those stitches with movement. He was going to have one hell of a scar. Like he'd escaped a hangman's noose. Dean tried not to shiver at the analogy. He supposed he had, in actuality. The final report from the doctor had sounded scarier than hell. Somehow, the bones protecting his passage hadn't collapsed, which would have crushed his airway. Sliced tendons that luckily weren't severed. A close call to the internal carotid artery. He'd come a hairsbreadth from bleeding to death. You can only sugarcoat *You almost died* so many ways.

Cade turned on the TV and let it play on low as he did stuff in the kitchen. Every now and then, Dean caught him watching only for him to quickly spin away. Hovering but trying to not look like he was.

"Dinner is soup, until you're more healed," Cade warned, joining him to sit on the couch.

Dean shrugged. He wasn't close to being hungry yet.

They watched TV until there was a knock on the door. Expecting the police, Dean was surprised his mother and father beat them to the house.

He sat up on the chair and hugged both, rubbing his mother's back as she choked on a couple breaths holding him.

Cade offered a pad and Dean started to write as they took seats.

I'm fine. Really. I'm waiting for the police so I'm not answering anything yet.

His mother nodded. "Okay." She and Trent shared a look. "We needed to talk to you anyway."

Dean arched an eyebrow. He wasn't expecting her to start the second she walked in the door again, but what she began to say couldn't have surprised him more.

"We've decided that it's not fair to make you uproot and leave. You have a wonderful man in your life, and he has a wonderful family."

Dean rested on a shoulder against the chair to study them. His parents held hands and they nodded in mutual agreement. This was definitely not the direction of conversation he would have expected from his folks. Cade had paused in the kitchen, not interrupting, just listening.

"We've decided since your father's retired there's no reason we can't move here. We want to be close to you, all of you." She looked toward Cade, including him.

Dean questioned his father with a blunt stare. *Why?*

"We started talking about it last night after you left," he confirmed. "We've missed having you close by, but after Daniel died we all kind of walled ourselves off." He grimaced. "It wasn't healthy and neither of us likes the distance. We miss you."

Dean twisted and found Cade, raising a hand to draw him into the conversation.

"I think that's a great idea. If it's feasible for you, I know the rest will be happy to call you family."

Dean's chest shuddered at Cade's unquestionable welcome. "Thank you," he mouthed for Cade.

Cade surprised him by leaning close and touching lips to forehead. Dean had no idea what had changed, but clearly *something* had with Cade.

"Good," Ann said. "It'll take a while, sell the house, stuff, but hopefully by summer? Does that sound like a good time to come?" She questioned both with an expectant gaze.

Cade smiled. "Should be. Silo is a good town."

"Do you mind if we stay for the police?" Trent asked.

Dean shook his head. He wrote on the pad then handed it over. *Better to only have to do this once.* He didn't doubt they were all going to have the same basic questions, anyway.

"Have you eaten? It's soup but I have plenty."

"We'd be happy to stay," Ann replied.

Dean grinned, hiding it. Cade was making buckets of points with his mother now.

Within the hour, Sheriff Archer and the case detective investigating the attacks on Dean arrived. They all sat around Cade's kitchen table as one by one Dean answered questions, placing the previous night into context of time with his evening.

"Can we keep this as your written statement?" the detective asked, holding Dean's pages when he was finished.

Dean nodded. He signed his name at the bottom and dated it.

"I'll make sure a copy gets into the Cassan files," the detective said, placing them with his other papers.

"Did you ever find out what happened to the power?" Cade asked.

"The main breaker outside had been turned off," Kelly informed them.

"Who was it?" his father asked.

"Wasn't there something tying them to Daniel?" Cade added. Dean was also wondering about that.

The detective flipped through notes. "The man behind all of this is Richie Spencer. His uncle, Jacob Tolleson was the man who shot Daniel. He died in prison two months ago of a heart attack."

"So it's all been for revenge? Payback?" Ann asked, appalled.

"It does look that way right now," he concurred. "He's still being questioned about the attacks on Dean and the fire. His personal vehicle matches the tire imprints taken from the day of the roof collapse, fingerprints from the first break-in prove that was him as well, and he has no alibi for the night of the fire. Last night added attempted murder. We think he's going to plead mentally unstable, but we're already prepared for that with the motivation behind the fire following his uncle's passing, and *then* ramping that up to physical harm. He's in jail, and not going anywhere."

"So it's just a matter of making sure it's all neat to prosecute?" Cade said.

"Mostly," the detective asked. He stood and offered a hand across the table. "Thank you very much for taking the time. I know it's got to be tiring after last night."

Dean motioned, *I'm okay.*

"I guess it's too soon to think of being Frankenstein for Halloween," Kelly said, teasingly.

Dean's groan was rough. He snatched the pad and scribbled. *Good thing I think you're a friend.*

Kelly read it and laughed. "I try to be." He handed it back. "I'll be checking back in a few days."

"And I have your phone numbers if I think of anything else," the detective offered. Dean walked them both to the door. He waited until they were both in their respective cars, then shut the door.

"I'm proud of you, babe," Cade whispered from behind him. Strong arms encircled his waist and pulled him into a solid chest.

He tried to turn around but was held fast. "After your parents leave, then we'll talk, okay?" Cade said right beside his ear.

Dean relaxed into the comforting hold and nodded.

* * * *

Cade led Dean to the couch after dinner and sat first, tugging him to sit in the cradle of his legs. Ann and Trent were gone, with promises and plans already being made. They were flying back to Michigan in the morning. They knew there was nothing else they could do, and if they wanted to be here by summer, that was only a few months away.

It was going to take some adjustments to having Dean's parents around but they'd get there. There was time to make those adjustments.

First, he had to grovel to the man in his embrace.

He stroked Dean's forearm, pushing the sweater sleeve he wore out of the way to reach skin.

"I know I keep saying it, but I want you to understand, I mean it, with all that I am. I'm sorry."

Dean nuzzled temple to temple. Cade knew the inability to talk left pretty much everything up to him at the moment.

"I have no excuse for not taking the impact the bond would have on you into consideration. I don't regret doing it. Never in a million years. I am regretting letting it happen the way it did." He had no excuses, and offered none. He should have had better control of his baser wants and the wolf's instincts. Losing his head in the heat of the moment was definitely no excuse.

Dean grasped a hand and dovetailed their fingers together, squeezing once.

Cade took that to mean that Dean understood. He wasn't fighting to get away, and while he was alert, he wasn't physically tense where they pressed together.

Cade tried to put his thoughts together to make coherent sense. His entire world had collapsed in a matter of hours last night. Every time he thought he was rebuilding something stronger, it turned into a house made of cards because he was still hiding from and avoiding the most intrinsic element necessary.

Himself.

He snuggled close, his lips brushing over Dean's ear. "You had every right to be mad last night. I haven't been explaining things well. Jamie pointed that out."

Dean reached for the pad and wrote a line. Cade read it over his shoulder as he did.

"I accept the wolf," Cade read out loud. Cade held him close, his frame literally trembling as the import of that one statement filled him. "I can't even put it to words how grateful I am that you do. That's not something anyone can prepare for."

He let out a slow breath. Time to be honest, with the both of them.

"What you said last night..." He kissed Dean's ear when Cade started to feel him tense, his spine pushing into Cade's chest. "You're right. I haven't been able to say I'm gay. I haven't wanted to. What I do know is I'm attracted to you. Now, don't be angry, but I want to explain this as fully as I can, okay?"

Dean hesitated, then nodded.

"I saw you, but didn't, that first night at the bar. That night, I was a wreck and I knew it. When I tried to walk away that was when the wolf slapped me. So I've been saying the wolf chose you, but that's not true. He didn't. I did." He locked his arms and curled around Dean to show him how wrong he'd been. He waited, only feeling Dean's patient expectation. "I chose you first as a friend. I chose to know you. I wanted you to meet my family. I knew what I was doing even if I wasn't aware then that I was also attracted to you. Then I found out you were gay and you became so much more dangerous."

Dean snickered, tilting to rest on Cade's shoulder to listen.

"Still comfortable?"

Dean nodded. The brace was bulky but it gave support Cade knew he needed.

"I want to be with you. Whatever anyone else wants to call it doesn't really matter. It's just me and you when you get to the barest bones." He took a slow breath. "What I'm saying is, I was just scared and I was being a coward to not accept that I can be in love with you." Because if he was, then that definitely meant he was in love with a man, and that was the battle he'd been waging.

But no more. It made absolutely no difference *what* it was called. It was what he *felt* that mattered. He'd seen that last night at Chris'.

Dean stiffened. He twisted and faced Cade as much as he could from between his thighs without spinning too far on his wounded neck.

"In love?" he rasped. "With me?"

"In love with you," Cade said. He caressed Dean's chin. "I was going to say exactly the same thing when I got here last night, if you'd have even opened the door. I was terrified you wouldn't talk to me. Last night made me realize that all the fuckups in the world won't keep me from feeling what I do for you. So gay or straight, sideways or hanging from a ceiling, I'm with you. Not because you're bonded or stuck with me, but because I love you."

Dean sighed roughly. He burrowed deeply into Cade's neck and wrapped an arm around his body to hold on as tight as he could.

"I know there are still things that need answered, that you have every right to ask." Cade ran a hand up and down his body. He'd do his best, always.

"Soon," Dean managed, pressed against his neck.

Cade agreed. He was confident once Dean had his voice back, they'd be sharing quite a few of these discussions between them.

They stayed like that on the couch for a while, enjoying the closeness. It was heaven. Looking at the clock below the TV a while later, he realized how late it was getting. After the last twenty-four hours, he was positive Dean was exhausted. "Want to get ready for bed?"

Dean sat up enough to look drowsily into Cade's eyes. Dean looked to already be half asleep. He was sure the medications he took at dinner were helping a lot to get him there. Leaning, Dean touched mouth to mouth. Cade didn't push for a deep kiss, letting Dean take what he wanted. When he moved away, Cade said, "And quit trying to talk. The doc said you needed time to heal the bruising to your vocal chords."

Dean rolled his eyes.

"Go get cleaned up."

"Thanks." No sound.

Cade smiled for him. He let Dean have a few minutes before heading to the bedroom himself, using the time to lock up. Dean was sitting in bed, a pad and pen on his lap when he got there.

After changing and brushing his teeth, Cade slipped in beside him. Dean was already writing. He took the pad when Dean handed it over.

Is that offer to move in still open?

"Of course."

He scribbled on the next line. *Is right now too soon?*

Cade laughed and turned a watchful Dean toward him with a palm. "Did you really think I was going to let you go back to Cassan after I just told you I love you?"

Dean's expression lightened and he rolled a shoulder.

"If you're really ready then yes, tomorrow we can bring whatever you want here."

Not what I would have planned, but yes.

"I know, babe." Cade nuzzled his temple. "Are you sore?"

A little. The stitches are uncomfortable. He dug his chin into the brace, as though punctuating the awkwardness.

"I'm sure they are," Cade replied after he'd written his answer. "I'll check them in the morning to change the bandage if you want."

Dean nodded. His gaze drew inward, thoughtful and a moment later, he started to write again. Cade waited him out, giving him time to say what he wanted.

When he handed it over, Dean cupped his ear, intimating he wanted to hear Cade.

"Okay." He focused on the writing. "I was fucking furious at you. —Got that," Cade quipped in retort. Dean smacked a knee to his leg with a dull thud. Cade jerked to laugh then started reading again. "You're right. It isn't gay, or not, but saying it the way you did made me believe you had no choice to be with me, a man."

Cade lowered the pad. "I know. That is one of those big things I'm so sorry for doing to you."

Dean tapped him to keep reading.

Cade swallowed and did as asked. "The bond was another one of those. I fully understand what you meant by it. I understand how that works in nature and I've had time to think it through. My question is can I bond you?"

Cade's voice trailed away as he read that silently again. He swore his eyes were lying to him. He'd *never* anticipated this happening. "You want to?" he whispered, unable to hide the enormity of his shock. He faced the man at his side, almost unable to form thoughts or words. Was Dean saying he loved Cade in return? Cade all but trembled at the gift he was getting from the man at his side.

Dean nodded, peeking through his lashes before reaching for the pad of paper. He wrote out something quickly. *If I'm stuck with you, then you are stuck with me, too.*

Cade chuckled, reading his tenacity and admiring him more for it. "Good point." Cade was almost finished with what Dean had written originally. "Lastly, why are you wearing pajamas?"

Cade's laughter deepened. "Because we're in bed and we're not doing more than sleeping until the doctor says you're healed enough." He needed Dean healed to erase the images of him bleeding on his kitchen floor. Watching him overnight in the hospital bed, those moments were about all he could envision on his eyelids.

Dean grumbled, though Cade saw the playfulness in his eyes. Just to give Cade a bit of hell.

Cade dropped the pad on the nightstand and turned out the small lamp. "Rest however you're most comfortable." He curled an arm around him to bring him down to the bed. He didn't doubt he was still going to screw things up, but he sincerely hoped he was done screwing up this part of it.

Chapter Eighteen

"You're sure he doesn't suspect?" Jamie asked, pinning the last ribbon to a chair outside.

Everything looked perfect. Jamie's talents were priceless. Chairs, ribbons, even the white wire arbor with ivy. Not flowers, and nothing excessive. The weather was holding, and aside from nerves, Cade couldn't believe he was doing this.

"Not a thing," Cade replied, getting back on track. "He thinks we're doing pictures for his parents."

"Evil."

Cade shrugged. Whatever worked. "I told him Chris had my suit so I was going to change here and to bring his mom and dad when he was ready." It gave everyone time to show up and hide their cars, too.

Jamie leaned close. "When are you doing the pack ceremony?"

"During the summer." It was part of why he wouldn't be expecting this. All the discussion had focused on that. "Was it hard?"

Jamie gave him a steady look. "It was...odd. Different, but I was never scared, either."

That eased some of Cade's deeper worries. "I think you're the first since Barbara to be honest. And now in just a year, we'll have two. You and Dean."

Jamie touched his forearm. "I'm honored."

Cade leaned and kissed his forehead. "Love you too, baby bro."

The back door popped opened. "I think they're here," Maya warned.

"Get everyone out of the house!" Jamie chirped.

Maya giggled but vanished in a whirl. A few seconds later, a deluge of people poured through the back door.

"That's everyone?"

Jamie counted heads. "Yep." Just then a knock on the front door rapped through the silence.

Jamie jumped and scooted out of the way. "Go!" He shoved Cade to go inside.

Cade shut the door and cleared the house to his soon to be husband and parents. "Hi. Come on in." He got a hug from Ann and shook Trent's hand. "The photographer is in the back if you want to go see what they've cooked up."

Ann just smiled and grasping her spouse's fingers, tugged him along.

Once they were out of earshot, Dean said, "Okay what's going on? Mom's been humming like a bee and even Dad has been smiling."

"Can't they just be happy that you are? To spend time with you?"

Dean arched an eyebrow, but finally relented. He leaned and got a quick greeting smooch, then ran his fingers over Cade's suit coat. "Damn, you look amazing."

"You do, too."

The back door opened. "The photographer is ready," his mother called.

"What kind of stuff are they going to do?" Dean asked, fixing Cade's tie.

"Oh, just some couples shots. I'm glad your parents could join us. We can do a few with them also."

"Mom would love that."

Cade almost cracked, but managed to hold it together to guide Dean through the house. At least he wasn't sweating. Not yet.

He opened the door and holding his breath, let Dean out first. He wished he could see Dean's expression. He heard it though in the rough indrawn breath and chuckle. "Oh, man. I've been had."

Coming up behind him, Cade spotted everyone turned in their seats, all with smiles.

"Want to get married today?" Cade whispered by his ear.

Dean swung around on his healed neck. "I thought... This summer?"

"That one is legit, but it's private," Cade said. Dean had only been to one pack run so far. Jamie had kept him company since his wounded throat had still made talking difficult then.

Cade moved to Dean's shoulder and clasped his hand. "I'm marrying *you*, now and here, because I love you. I don't want you to ever doubt that."

Dean swallowed. Hard. "Yes."

Cade chuckled. "Glad to get that part out of the way." Dean's eyes sparkled in the sunlight with the teasing. With a gentle tug and hand in hand, they walked together down the aisle.

Dean's voice was sure, if a little thick with emotion when he whispered the I do. His voice was deeper, rougher after the trauma he'd suffered. Neither they nor the doctor knew if it would ever return to normal. Cade didn't care one iota. It was sexier than ever, especially when he moaned or cried out Cade's name.

He felt Dean's hands grasp his and realized he'd lost himself in staring at the man in front of him.

"I do." A quiet chuckle from the closest seats proved it hadn't gone unnoticed.

He withdrew a box from his coat pocket and slipped one of the rings on Dean's hand, offering its mate for him to do the same.

"I now pronounce you husband and husband," the officiant said with warm delight. "You may share your first kiss as a couple."

Cade brought Dean close and literally felt his heart kick into his ribs when their lips met. Dean quivered and sighed.

"Love you," Cade said against his lips when they parted.

"I love you, too," Dean echoed, not so much as blinking to break the connection.

They faced the gathering of family and friends. Everyone stood and applauded. Dean's fingers gripped his. Cade *finally* felt like he could take a deep breath.

Dean stood at his side now in the kitchen as people milled through Chris' house. "Is this for real? What about the marriage license?"

Cade tugged him close. They'd taken photos for over half an hour and he needed something to drink, sipping on water after a champagne toast from Chris.

He felt his face warm. He wasn't the kind to blush, but he didn't doubt this time he was. "Remember that document I had you sign last week?" He'd slipped it under Dean's nose when he was distracted, getting him to sign it with hardly a look, telling him it was hospital stuff. Cade waited for Dean to nod. "You're official." It also helped to have friends and pack who knew how to get things done.

"Sneaky bastard."

Cade shrugged. "You have no idea how hard it was to keep this quiet."

Dean mused, obviously not put out by the deception. "He didn't do the Mr. and Mr. at the end."

Cade caressed a forearm with a light finger. "I wasn't going to presume."

"I'd be okay with Dean Eckler-Rose."

Cade swallowed the water on his tongue. Dean hadn't even hesitated. "You're sure? I—"

Dean shook his head, halting him. "It's just a name. Besides, when we have kids, never want them to doubt that they were wanted by both of us."

Cade almost melted into a puddle. "You mean it?"

"Mean it," he said before stealing a gentle kiss.

And as if to prove that Cade was being truthful, the officiant approached. "Is now okay?" He studied both questioningly.

Cade offered a hand. "The whole thing has been explained."

"Wonderful." He produced a book from behind him. "If you'd both please sign, I can get this copied and returned to you to file on Monday."

"Thanks, George. Really appreciate today. George Tennar, Dean Eckler-Rose." Cade introduced them.

Dean laughed and smiled, taking his hand and shaking as well. "You're a devious bunch."

"It's been a while since I've been part of a surprise wedding. They never get old."

"Has anyone ever run the other way?" Dean wondered, signing his name to the line, officially making him a married man.

"Not yet." George laughed.

"Stay and eat, George. I'm sure Jamie outdid himself."

"Thank you. I'll be here for a bit." He closed the book, protecting the page. "Congratulations again."

Cade wound an arm around Dean. "You should know, you took me by surprise from the beginning. The wolf just kept me from making a larger than life mistake," he said as he nuzzled into Dean's neck below his ear, keeping their conversation private.

"Oh?"

"He wouldn't let me walk away, and when I realized I was feeling something more, he finally shut up." Cade huffed. "Now I'm never letting you go."

"Not gonna happen," Dean concurred. He tapped the ring on his finger.

"Are you disappointed in today?"

"Not at all," Dean replied. "This is actually perfect. This was something I never wanted to plan. I wanted to find the right guy, but this?" he said. He rocked a hand toward the melee in the house. "Not my forte." He smiled for Cade. "And you've absolutely won over my mother with this."

"Long hair and all, huh?" Cade teased warmly.

Dean smiled. "And all."

Cade grazed from below his ear to find his lips, savoring the first kiss of many.

About the Author

Diana DeRicci is the sexy, flirty pen name of Diana Castilleja. A romance author at heart, DeRicci's writing takes you into a saucier spectrum of sensuality and sexual adventure, where a happily-ever-after is still the key to any story. Diana lives in Central Texas with her husband, one son, and a feisty little Chihuahua named Rascal. You can catch the latest news on all of Diana DeRicci's writing and books on her website. Feel free to drop Diana an email. She'd love to hear from you.

Visit her on the web at:
www.DianaDeRicci.com

PURPLE SWORD PUBLICATIONS LLC
Romantic Speculative Fiction
www.purplesword.com